Faithless Friends and Replacement Lovers

Short Stories about Love and Loss

Elizabeth Horst

Elizabeth's Writing Corner
Myrtle Beach, SC
https://www.elizabethswritingcorner.com

To Him—

Faithful have you always been
A loyal Friend through and through
While others may be Replaced
There's no other Love like you.

Table of Contents

A Note from the Author

We all wish for our own happily ever after. Yet, doesn't it often feel just out of reach? Or, perhaps, we might reach a rare place where we look around and see happiness and contentment on all sides, but then we do something to royally screw up the situation for ourselves! What an awkward but perfectly normal and human predicament to be in.

I wrote these short stories many years ago when facing similar situations that the characters in these pages will demonstrate to you. As I learned, the capacity in which others fill the roles of friend or lover in our lives vary greatly. Some are but a mere daydream while others are as real and shocking as a cup of ice-cold water poured upon the head.

No matter what role the people in my life may have filled and for whatever length of time, I am thankful for each one who has crossed my path. I'm even more grateful for those who are still in my life and have not been afraid to stay with me throughout the confusion, heartache, and difficulty along the way.

My wish is that these stories will inspire you and provoke you to think about your own life where relationships are concerned. Yet, try not to focus on the type of people that you have encountered on your own journey but think more about the type of friend and lover that you have chosen to be. The choice is always ours to make, whether we will be fleeting and false or faithful and true, and every new day brings the opportunity to be our best self.

To life and to love,

Elizabeth Horst

November 2025

Chapter One

Rosalyn and Her Father the General

Rosalyn Novotny's father was a bear of a man. Not quite literally, but he was tall, dark, and imposing with a deep growl of a voice and a commanding presence. It was fitting that he had spent most of his life as an army commander, having risen through the ranks in his youth during the brutal years of war. Now, he lived comfortably while the country enjoyed a period of tentative peace.

Rosalyn stared at herself in the looking glass in her bedroom, having just let down her hair, which was a great black mass of curls. She always imagined her hair was exactly like her father's, if he had also worn his own locks long and unshorn instead of in one great mass on the top of his head.

Feeling hatred for herself due to her close resemblance to her bear of a father, she quickly bound the curls back up and covered her head once more. It was already past bedtime, but she stayed up a bit longer, her candle still lit in case she decided to sleep downstairs in the servants' quarters.

Her grandmother, her father's mother, was already sleeping in the big bed in her room. It was Rosalyn's own bed, but she had been required to give it up once its current occupant arrived for a familial visit. The curtains were drawn securely around the bedposts so the sleeping woman would not be awakened by the flickering of the candle.

Rosalyn could instinctively imagine her grandmother's shrill voice slicing through the quiet. "Put out the candle and go to bed, child!"

She glanced over at the smaller bed opposite where her grandmother slept and sighed. Leaning down, she blew out the flame and climbed up quietly among the pillows and sheets, sitting there with her knees pulled up to her chin in a most unladylike fashion.

It was not as if she feared her grandmother. That old woman was more annoying than fearsome. Her father, on the other hand, was both terrible and terrifying, but now that her grandmother was here, she was safe. At the same time, however, she regarded her grandmother with the same hatred and respect that she bestowed upon her father.

Grandmother Novotny had arrived several years ago, shortly after Rosalyn had turned twelve. She had been horrified to see how the girl had been brought up by the gypsy servant woman, Lizaveta. Grandmother immediately banned Rosalyn from going into the gypsies' quarters and forbade the servants from being in the great house when not conducting their regular duties. Then, Grandmother prevented Rosalyn from helping with the common housework and forced her to take up the womanly craft of needlework.

The only things pleasing to Grandmother about Roslyn were that she was quiet, attentive, and loved to read. Yet, even Rosalyn's most attractive traits only went so far, as Grandmother also found her silence rather ominous at times, her quiet submission a cover-up for a rebellious spirit, and her reading a poor excuse to learn about revolutionary matters that were only for men to explore and discuss.

In truth, Rosalyn had no interest in rebellion or politics. She was simply curious about the company of her father and his army leaders. Since her childhood, she had developed a habit of hiding behind the drapes in the hall beside the dining room where the men took their dinner. The more they ate and drank, the more they talked and the louder they swore.

Rosalyn could remember being quite young and feeling all alone in the house one night as she stood behind the drapes, listening to the wild commotion going on before her. That night, just as the rowdiness began to reach its peak, Roslyn had suddenly felt a hand upon her shoulder. Now, she smiled to think about how violently she had started before realizing that it was only Lizaveta.

"You better go to bed, dear," Lizaveta had said in her thick accent. When Rosalyn simply looked up at the servant with wide eyes, the woman smiled. "Get your night things and you can stay with the children."

Rosalyn had been only too happy to comply. She loved the gypsies and often wished she could be one of them. They were the only family she knew. Lizaveta was the housekeeper, and her husband Dmitry was the gardener and caretaker. They had five children, and others from the little gypsy community frequently came in and out of the house as well. They all loved Rosalyn and affectionately called her Rosie, even while still respecting her as a young woman of the upper class.

Rosalyn sighed, crawled between the sheets, and lay down. Now that Grandmother Novotny seemed intent on staying with them forever, long gone were her happy times of daily life with the gypsies. She often wondered what fate would have befallen her had her grandmother not come, or had her father not been so odious, or—most of all—had her mother not died of a fever when Roslyn was still an infant.

Her mother. The word sounded so foreign. Rosalyn wanted to get up at that moment, light the candle once again, and go down to the parlor where her mother's picture hung upon the flowered wallpaper. Her mother was a beautiful lady with deep brown eyes, smooth peachy skin, and flowing light brown hair, almost appearing as if she were a foreigner from the West.

Rosalyn had occasionally visited her mother in the parlor throughout her childhood, but her curiosity had especially grown stronger in the last few years. She remembered how Lizaveta found her in the forbidden room just last week after Rosalyn had slipped in without permission and stood before the picture as if lost in a daydream. Yet, the kindly house servant never scolded.

Instead, Lizaveta told Rosalyn in her broken accent, "You look like your mama, more and more every day."

Rosalyn was surprised by that. But then she caught a look at herself in the mirror and said angrily in Liza's own tongue, "Not with my ugly bear hair!"

"Your hair is beautiful, Rosie," Liza answered gently, but the kindly woman could do nothing to correct Rosalyn's thinking that she was condemned to be a cruel combination of her angelic mother and demonic father. For too long, Rosalyn had imagined that, despite her face resembling her mother's, her heart was as black as her father's treatment of her. And, as if to prove it, her hair grew blacker and curlier with every passing year.

In fact, the more Rosalyn grew and matured, she began to hate herself for any similarities she imagined that she shared with her mother. She sensed that every time her father returned home on leave with fresh injuries, he seemed to notice the similarities as well. Even though he never spoke his thoughts aloud and never treated her any differently, Rosalyn often found her father staring at her in a most probing and curious way.

She was not bold enough to admit it, but Rosalyn often wished to hear directly from her father. Unfortunately, her father never spoke to her without giving an order, since that was all he was good for. Neither did he ever touch his own daughter, whether for ill or for good. While he provided for her in terms of goods, education, and material necessities, she was a lonely child with few friends or entertainment. As far as General Notovny had ever been concerned, his child was simply a fixture of the house, and he would hardly have minded if she were just another gypsy.

General Novotny's war ailments most often worsened before they improved, which made his irascible temper all the worse this time around. Whenever his mother was out and about socializing, Notovny was a living terror to all the house. Prone to fits and rages, his every wish became a command, and no one dared to suggest he act otherwise.

After the last harsh winter mellowed into a mild spring and another tentative war settlement was reached, he seemed to relax somewhat, but the occupants of the house never let their guard down. Only Grandmother remained oblivious to his foul moods and violent temper, for he took care to restrain his anger in her presence.

As spring turned into summer, Rosalyn turned fourteen and her father suddenly seemed affable toward her. He would command her in an almost imploring tone to read him stories in the evenings, for his eyesight was failing from spending so much time in the bright sunlight on snowy marches that he could no longer read for himself.

Rosalyn always complied, out of fear, but she hated it. She knew from Liza's stories that her mother often read to her father before she had been born and before he had been called away on war business. Whenever Grandmother was not around to hear her new and dreadful habit, Rosalyn began to read with a lisp that resembled some of the peculiarities found in the accents of the gypsies.

As if that was not enough, she added an occasional dry cough to further irritate her father. She knew that he hated any type of cough that reminded him of his own nights of sickness, so she purposefully did it as often as possible, until one night he threw the nearest fire iron at her and commanded her to leave. Rosalyn left promptly, with relief and a distinctly evil feeling of satisfaction.

After that, all attempts at civility on her father's part fell away. He addressed her with harsh words, cursing and mocking her at every opportunity, particularly before Dmitry and Lizaveta. He told her she was useless and, most cruelly of all, blamed her for her mother's death.

Rosalyn always held her tongue in her father's presence and dared not complain to Grandmother about the abuse. In her own mind, however, her fury had no limits. Secretly, she did not blame her father, for she blamed herself for her mother's death. Yet, her own hatred for him continued to grow, and she refused to speak to him. On the rare occasion that she permitted herself to mention him, Rosalyn formally referred to him as "my father the general."

One afternoon, the week before her tutor came back for the next school session, Grandmother suddenly announced she had business elsewhere and departed in a flurry of activity. Around the same time, Rosalyn discovered a book in the library about a rebellious young woman who forsook the teachings of her parents and tutors to live wildly and in whatever manner she wished.

As was typical for novels of their time, this story was quite long with a winding plot that stretched longer than the Volga, and it was entitled The Insubordinate Daughter, and What Became of Her. Rosalyn devoured as much of the novel as she could that day and throughout the night as well, wasting two whole candles in the process.

The next day, she was exhausted but in a state of nervous anticipation to know the rest of the story. Her tutor, finding her attentive but unable to focus on her assignments properly, requested a private meeting with her father at the end of the second hour. When Novotny consented, the thin and balding man informed the general, "Miss Rosalyn Novotny has unfortunately fallen into a state of love."

Her father, not bothering to investigate the matter, was furious and sent Rosalyn to bed immediately without tea, supper, or even dinner, and commanded the tutor to return on the following day. Rosalyn was immensely pleased by the punishment, for it provided her with ample time to finish the book.

Unfortunately, the exhausted young woman fell asleep during a slow chapter where the heroine plotted revenge against a kind, humble servant girl who had done nothing to deserve it.

When she awoke nearly six hours later, Rosalyn found tea nearby on the nightstand, but her book was gone. Rising in distraction, she called for Lizaveta, but there was no reply. She went to the door and tried the handle, but it was locked. She searched the room for her book, but to no avail. Having no other recourse but to wait for freedom to arrive in the morning, Rosalyn sat on the bed and plotted her revenge over cold tea and crumpets.

After finishing her plans, she went to the window and looked out. She could see the gypsy village over the hills, the little lights blinking on as the evening dusk began to fall. She sat there among the drapes for quite a while in silence until the whole room inside was as dark as the night outside. She considered going back to bed at that point, but just then she heard the lock sliding back and the door slowly opening. It was Lizaveta with a candle in her hand.

Rosalyn felt a pang as she watched the woman approach her bed, obviously coming to check on her.

"Rosie?" the woman called softly, seeing the bed intact and the tea completed but the girl nowhere in sight.

"Here," Rosalyn replied just as quietly, rising from her seat by the window.

The woman set the candle down by the bed and approached Rosalyn. "You should forgive your father. My husband told me about new threats in the area, and I am sure your father is troubled by the possibilities. He did not mean anything by his unkindness."

"My father the general never means anything by his unkindness where I am concerned," Rosalyn said stiffly, in her own language.

"You will forgive him, then?" Liza asked, taking the girl's hands in hers in a gesture of affection.

Rosalyn sighed and looked up at the only kind mother figure she had ever known. "I am thirsty and tired," she said in the gypsy tongue. "Can I stay with the children?"

Liza smiled and nodded, turning to pick up the candle and the tea tray. She motioned Rosalyn to follow her and they went downstairs in silence.

It was not until they reached the entryway to the servants' quarters that Rosalyn remembered.

Stopping Lizaveta with a hand on her elbow, she looked up at the woman and asked, "Why did you take my book away?"

Liza looked down at the girl quietly. Then she smiled sadly.

"You are a lot like your mother, Rosie. She was a free spirit, too, and it hurt her when she was not careful." Then she added plainly, "I hid it so your father would not see what you were reading."

Rosie felt surprised, having thought previously that Lizaveta was unable to read. "Did you read it?"

Liza shook her head. "But I can read what it is doing to you." Then she took the girl by the hand and led her into the house.

Shortly thereafter, Novotny was called back to the border for six months. The household returned to how Rosalyn loved it best, but she did not forget her plans. When her father returned in the late spring in a bad temper and with an even weaker vision, she knew that time was short. He began to drink more, and his fits and rages became more common. Rosalyn still remained civil to him, but she often felt like screaming back at him and hurling the samovar at his ugly face.

Then, without warning, Grandmother Novotny returned, taking over the daily affairs of the house once again and keeping a strict eye on Rosalyn's actions. Rosalyn feared that this turn of events might derail her carefully laid plans, yet she clung to the hope that a window of opportunity would open and allow her to act.

The next day, Grandmother Novotny spent the morning supervising the household chores as usual while overseeing Rosalyn's sewing and schooling. The hours and minutes seemed to creep by, but finally, it was time for tea.

Rosalyn waited for her grandmother's careful inspection of her needlework before going upstairs to her room, carefully packing a bag with simple clothing and other belongings. Then she washed her face, put on a fresh apron, and went downstairs for tea. She behaved herself so perfectly throughout the hour that Grandmother Novotny was impressed.

"Child, you must come with me this afternoon," she announced, beginning to discuss the itinerary for the day to visit her extensive social circle.

Upon hearing the plans, Rosalyn suddenly paled and shivered from a cold chill. "Grandmother," she politely asked, "might I rest in bed this afternoon instead?"

Grandmother was surprised by that request, rising and coming around the table to inspect the young lady. After a careful examination of her face, neck, and eyes, the matter was settled.

"You are ill," Grandmother said in a disappointed tone. "Yes, you shall stay in bed for the afternoon, and through the evening as well. No wonder you seemed so compliant today!" Commanding her upstairs, Grandmother was soon on her way, leaving Rosalyn alone for the afternoon.

As soon as the old woman went out, Rosalyn rose and went to the window, watching the carriage disappear around the bend in the road. When she turned from the window, she saw Lizaveta watching her with wise eyes.

"I will be in the parlor," Rosalyn said quietly. On the threshold, however, she paused and looked back. "May I please have the book back?" she asked.

A flicker of uncertainty crossed Liza's face, but then she said quietly, "It is under the middle cushion of the sofa."

"Thank you," Rosie said happily and ran toward the parlor without further hesitation.

Coming around the corner, Rosalyn nearly collided with her father, who had just descended the stairs. They both came to a quick halt and stared at one another without a word, both of them considering the unexpected situation.

Rosalyn was the first to break the silence. "Grandmother has gone out," she announced. "Shall I read to you in the parlor?"

"No," her father growled, turning away from her and his mind intent on other business. Then he glanced back. "Put a book on my desk for later."

Feeling a great sense of victory, Rosalyn ran to do his bidding. Finding the book where Lizaveta had said it would be, she sat down immediately and found the chapter that had been running through her mind that whole day. She had not read the entire book but distinctly remembered the portion in which the heroine had decided to run away.

Sticking her finger in the particular chapter, Rosalyn ran upstairs and placed it on her father's desk. There were loose papers all around, so she took one and put it in the place she hoped her father would notice. Then she went across the hall to her room, taking up her bag and returning to her father's room.

Behind the general's bed hung heavy drapes, concealing a doorway that led to a second-story porch. Rosalyn went to this door now, slipping behind the drapes and waiting to see what would happen next.

Several minutes later, she heard the steps creaking and peeked out through a slit in the drapes to see her father sitting down heavily at his desk. Taking up his thick spectacles, he put them on and took up the book. Apparently, he recognized the cover and the title from some ago time, for he immediately swore, threw down the volume, and rose up with a shout.

Rosalyn's brow wrinkled as she opened the door behind her.

"Goodbye, my Father the General," she said quietly, her voice hidden behind the drapes and covered by the angry shouting.

She slipped away down the stairs and changed her clothes in the woods, hiding all of her belongings that would betray her true class. Examining her appearance in a nearby pool of water, she was satisfied and took up her small pack, setting out for a new life in the gypsy camp.

Rosalyn was certain she could make her own way in the world with the gypsies, for they already knew who she was and readily accepted her into the village. The only thing she wondered was how soon it would be until Lizaveta would come to check on her and if the woman would force her to return home.

After a week with no message from Liza, Rosalyn's thoughts of her old life began to fade entirely. Before she could become established in the new community, however, war returned to the area and the camp had to be disbanded. Most of the village retired to their winter quarters close to town, but the more mobile of them packed up to follow the army and serve where needed. Rosalyn went with the adventurous gypsies, wondering why she went, and curious to see if she would see her father.

Weeks of hard life on the field went by, and Rosalyn learned to work like the rest of them as cooks, water carriers, cleaners, nurses, and more. The gypsies knew the army nearly as well as they knew themselves. Rosalyn knew her father was not present, for the highest rank there was only a captain. She knew which soldiers were kind, which were cruel, which ones knew about her existence, and which ones did not.

There was one young soldier in particular, a guard for the left flank, that she knew was acutely aware of her presence. She wondered what his name was, though she knew his last name from the embroidered patch on his coat, and she wondered how old he was.

One afternoon, after a busy morning of setting up camp on a side hill, Rosalyn was resting alone by a tree. She sighed from weariness, relieved for the moment of rest.

Hearing a sound behind her, she quickly peeked around the tree and then rose, her eyes widening in surprise to see the young guard before her. Rosalyn gazed back at him, plainly and unashamedly, but neither made a move for some time.

After a moment, he stepped closer, but then she spoke quietly to him in the tongue reserved for the upper class, "Do not touch me."

He instantly recoiled, staring in astonishment to learn that she was nobility, on the same level as he. Then he was embarrassed and ashamed.

"I didn't know—how did you—I thought you—how did you become one of the gypsies?"

Rosalyn turned away from him and sat back down. When the guard continued to babble incoherent phrases, she looked up at him.

"Are you on duty?" she asked.

"No," he said shortly.

"Then sit down and stop gabbling like an old goose."

He complied wordlessly as the silence stretched between them. She found it comfortable, but a glance in his direction told her that he was still embarrassed and uneasy.

"Do you want to leave?" she asked quietly.

"Do you want me to leave?" he returned, gazing at her.

Rosalyn felt a sudden nervous prickle but shook her head, and he stayed.

After that, they met often. Things still felt awkward between them for quite some time, but eventually, Rosalyn began to feel more at ease with the young soldier.

His name was Alex. He was warm, kind, and much different than any other man she had met before. The first time he touched her hand, she felt a curious sensation that caused her to tremble so unexpectedly that she was concerned for her well-being. After that, she deliberately kept herself at a distance from him, half-afraid of him, half-afraid of herself.

One night, as she lay down to sleep, she heard the voice of her old tutor in her head: "Miss Rosalyn Novotny has unfortunately fallen into a state of love."

She sighed and wondered if it was true.

The next day, Rosalyn met Alex when he was on duty and asked him, "Are you in love with me?"

He was standing and facing the camp, his gun slung over his shoulder as he ate a pie she had brought him. He looked down at her and smiled slightly, as if he was amused by the questioning of a mere child.

"Well? Are you?" she demanded impatiently.

His smile turned a bit sad as he shook his head, taking another bite of pastry and meat.

Rosalyn was not surprised by his answer, but she felt a pang of sadness.

After a moment, Alex looked at her. "If you were another girl, I would fall in love with you in an instant," he told her in a low voice.

"Another girl?" she wondered, feeling another pang cross her heart.

He looked about carefully and then said to her in an even lower voice, "It is not right to love the only daughter of the general."

At that, Rosalyn felt flabbergasted, and strong sensations of anger, remorse, and bitterness followed in quick succession. She held her peace for several minutes, but finally told him, "I never chose my father the general."

"I'm sorry, Rosie," Alex said, reaching out. He was wearing a warm coat and thick knit gloves that she had made for him.

Rosalyn allowed him to embrace her and leaned into his strength momentarily. Then, she took his empty dish and left, knowing they would not talk again, and that she would miss him more than he would miss her.

The following week, the unit marched back into the village that they had left over a year ago. Despite being familiar with the sights of death and destruction, Rosalyn was shocked to see how everything had changed. Houses were gone, and new constructions were being raised in their places. People were gone, too, and other villagers dwelt in their stead.

Her grandmother, she learned, had fled the destruction long ago to live with her daughter. Her father was still a general, but with increasingly failing health and an equally failing reputation.

"What of Dmitry, Lizaveta, and the children?" Rosalyn asked the gossips.

At that, they fell silent before admitting that only Liza and two of her children remained. Dmitry had fallen in battle, and the three youngest children had perished in the plague.

Disheartened by the news, Rosalyn rushed to the center of town. When she reached the spot where her old house stood, however, she found the mansion demolished. Only the servants' quarters remained, and beside it, a new structure that seemed hastily thrown together.

Lizaveta saw her first and ran toward her, tears sparkling in her eyes. Rosalyn was too surprised by Liza's gray hair and wrinkles to say anything, but she held the woman closely and wondered at the fact that she stood a full three inches taller and could no longer rest her head on Liza's loving shoulder.

Hearing a door creaking, Rosalyn turned to see an old man stumbling out of the new construction and blinking painfully in the bright sun.

"Hello, Father," Rosalyn said stoically to the shell of the bear.

He started upon hearing her voice but then looked at Lizaveta. "Liza?" he commanded, his voice a mere croak. "Who is that?"

"It is Rosalyn," the woman said simply, gazing at the young woman with a broad smile. "Rosie has come home."

CHAPTER TWO

The Noblewoman's Dilemma

There once was a young noblewoman of tall stature who possessed a great heart underneath the sternest of visages. She had faced many trials and tribulations of both soul and body in her few short years, and yet the challenges she had encountered only served to make her more forthwith and charming in all of her endeavors. But the greatest of trials was still yet to come.

It all began one fine summer day when a man of royalty who hailed from the Germanic north arrived in her kingdom by the sea with a party of young folk intent on serving the lost souls of the city. Now, our young noblewoman, the

Lady Honora, was devoted to service, and so she naturally found herself in association with the regal party, and
yet she kept herself distant and reserved the whole while.

In the greatest of ironies, while she tightly withheld
her own passions with one hand, she extended her other
hand of mercy, unflinchingly demanding that every soul
reveal to her the deepest sensations of their own tender
hearts.

Truly, it was the greatest of ironies, and yet it was a
perfectly sensible response for such a noblewoman in
her place of standing, for she was greatly compassionate
but held herself to the most rigid of standards. That is to
say, by means of a practical example, while quite familiar
with and receptive to the passion of grief, Lady Honora
only permitted the sunlight of mirth to chink her armor
in the most advantageous of situations and among the
most trusted of intimates.

Enter then the particular fellow who led the stalwart
company of servants. Lord Archibald was such a one that
beamed of mirth and leaped high upon the face of the
earth on frequent occasion with lightning-fast shoes that
carried him far and wide. Our poor noblewoman had never
quite encountered one of such wit and mettle, and yet she

was immediately won over by his kindness and generosity against her better judgment.

"Aha," said her wise old professor, enthroned upon the tower of learning when he was not traveling far and wide in pursuit of souls to join his school of sages.

"He hails from a land beside the long, tidal river," the young noblewoman said judiciously, referencing a country from the north as she stood before her tutor of many years, standing as straight in her youth as he was bent over from the multiplicity of years.

"He would, I reckon, carry me straight off into the sunset, though he has no steed of valor, and stands as thin and beanly as a scarecrow that ran away from his own cornfield, save for his great mop of hair that puts Prince Absalom to shame."

"His great mop of hair, as you so aptly put it, my lady," interjected one of the nobles that regularly sat at her table for sup, "is a beautiful work of art that rivals only your own, my lady."

"Well," the noblewoman replied reproachfully, "such things are of a vain and vaporous substance to speak of. I prefer to speak upon the matters of the heart." Here, she looked once more at the sage elder graciously and extended a compassionate hand to him in order to assist him.

"Matters of the heart," the tutor replied ponderously, gazing at Lady Honora with a probing eye. "You manly lady! You shut up your own heart like a chest of drawers with never a key in sight!"

"What a crooked remark!" reproachfully exclaimed the noblewoman's favorite handmaiden that evening as Lady Honora gave a retelling of the day's events before sleep.

"Nay, but my aged professor is true," Honora said wearily, "and after many moons of imparting knowledge and wisdom to me, he ought to know. It is the way of our people, and you know this to be true."

The handmaiden appeared curious but also bewildered, being more familiar with the rough speech of the peasantry class than the cryptic words of the noble lords and ladies. "Then what shall you do? Shall you choose your gallant lord who joyfully wishes for your hand, or will you focus your energies only upon the meditation of the grievous hard times that the earth must endure?"

At that, Honora appeared to soften slightly as she lay her head upon the pillow. "My gallant lord, as you call him, is an oasis of peace in a mad world. He has ventured back north to make ready his preparations and then shall return to our land to hear my answer."

"Truly, he is worthy of a good answer," the maiden said with a smile, drawing the coverlet over her lady and retreating to the door with her candle. Pausing in the doorway, she boldly added, "Perhaps you would do best to put your sensitivities aside and elope with him. Goodnight, my lady."

Honora smiled at the fanciful thought brought on by her maiden's impertinent remark and shook her head with amusement as she drifted off to sleep. Yet, upon waking the next day, her qualms returned, and she immediately shut herself in her room with her best books of learning and a great helping of the finest crisps made from the ripest of all vegetable roots.

Several maidens checked in on Lady Honora at various and sundry times, but she was always found fast asleep upon the bed or rigidly seated upright with a book on her lap and tears upon her cheeks. In short, she was distracted from the world with her dilemma and truly as terrible as an army with banners.

At last, the day came that the man of choice arrived on the scene, as grand a spectacle as any, with his face bearing a great smile and his curly locks disheveled by the wind. He waited before the threshold of the great house with expectation and delight, sending word to the Lady Honora of his return following his successful journey.

The messenger flew with winged steps both elated and tremulous, and soon a great gathering stood outside the door of the noblewoman's chamber. There was a noisome chatter amongst the good folk, full of rumors and assumptions, but it immediately died away as soon as Honora's foot tread upon the threshold.

All faces turned to her expectantly and all ears were peeled for a word from her gracious lips. The noblewoman looked compassionately toward the host gathered, then toward the open door where the courtyard lay beyond with the fine nobleman awaiting her response to accompany him.

"What then, fair lady?" cried out an impatient voice. "What is your answer? What shall you say?"

Lady Honora looked around the group momentarily and then gazed toward the doorway, a distracted smile lighting up her features. She gave her reply by uttering just one phrase: "My Archibald!"

CHAPTER THREE

The Preposterous Proposal

A long time ago in Bonny Old England, there was a fine but rather preposterous knight named Sir John Sebastian Dudley. His most defining characteristic was demonstrating a great fluctuation of emotions in a way not at all befitting a man of his stead. Oftentimes, he found himself in perilous scraps because of his inability to control his fits, rages, whims, and fancies. Other times, he neatly escaped by the mere kindness of his comrades and boasted that it was he who had rescued himself from peril by his own wit and merit.

In the springtime of his thirtieth year, Sir Dudley was called to the front line of battle for his king. After settling his affairs and preparing for the journey in obedience to the throne, he rode off on his most trusted steed with many a romantic thought about how gloriously he would bring the war to a victorious close for his country.

Shortly after his departure, Dudley chanced to fall into company with a group of excellent fellows on a dangerous mission of which they would speak nothing. Pressed by curiosity, Dudley was determined to learn something of their secret quest and thus plagued the group every day with various and sundry offers of service.

For a whole week, the noble company rebuffed Dudley's unsubtle suggestions, but they soon tired of his fanciful words and plotted a scheme to rid themselves of him altogether. As they expected to arrive upon the scene of war within three days' time, the excellent group swiftly set their plot in motion by inviting Dudley to give particular care and attention to a young fellow in their company who would not be directly engaged in battle.

At first, Sir Dudley felt offended at their offer, thinking he was far better than acting the nursemaid to an inexperienced youth who was sure to flee at the first sign of a bloody skirmish. After further consideration, however, he recalled how deliberately the group of nobles respected the young fellow. Presuming this was due to the lad having a prestigious background, Dudley concluded that any good deed done for the young man would certainly result in a bountiful reward.

From there, Dudley was all too happy to comply with the group's wishes, promising to bear young O'Reilly henceforth in safety. Having succeeded at their plot, the noblemen bid a hearty farewell to the young fellow and beat a hasty retreat, leaving Dudley and O'Reilly quite to themselves.

As it was nearing evening, Dudley suggested they make camp for the night, offering to take care of the fire and nightly sup while pointing out a fine grassy spot for the young noble to take his rest. O'Reilly complied in silence, spending much of the evening in quiet reflection and waiting until the sun had gone down to remove his armor and bid Dudley a good night.

Upon the morrow, the two fellows resumed their travels, making quite a motley pair and creating a fine topic for gossip as they wound through the little villages and towns toward the scene of battle. Indeed, a goodly number of villagers and townsfolk wondered at their appearance, for the two diligently rode by at a rapid pace without a single word to one another or to anyone else, putting their poor horses at danger of wearing down before they even reached the war.

On Dudley's part, he felt sorely irritated at O'Reilly for being a measly fellow without the stomach for good food, fine drink, and comfortable living. After all, Dudley had awoken with a fine thought and presented it to his companion.

"Let us ride far today, my good man, and tonight we will dine in comfort and sleep at the finest of inns in Millersville," he told O'Reilly as they saddled up for the day.

"Nay, but we will follow the main road through Dunshire and arrive at battle by noon tomorrow," O'Reilly replied, wise to Dudley's scheme to bypass the poverty-stricken towns and head further north than necessary.

The two knights, thus being at odds, spent much of the day in silence. Upon reaching the crossroads leading to a westerly road or the northern path, the pair came to a halt and Dudley began to wheedle.

"Think ye about the goodly time we would have, what with the fine inn owned by my friend Alan and his kin. What has any scurvy town by comparison but a rowdy lot that would surely meet your disdain?"

"We shall go on as planned, for 'tis on the main path leading to the west, and we may surely camp solitary if the company displeases you," O'Reilly said without hesitation, his youthful voice certain beneath his helmet.

Growling in irritation, Dudley jerked his horse's head in the intended direction and returned to his former silence for the remainder of the day. Only when they reached the last village just beyond the battlefield did he recover his tongue, doing his best to find merriment in food and drink that evening.

As for O'Reilly, while his companion found solace from the upcoming conflict in strong liquor and deep sleep, this young fellow was occupied in more noble preparations, much to the admiration of the others present.

The morning sun rose early and red in the eastern sky, bidding the two knights rise and join the king's army in battle. O'Reilly remained as cheerful and complacent as always as they broke their fast, loaded their goods upon O'Reilly's horse, and went forward on foot, but Dudley was in quite an irascible temper.

"I tell you," Knight Dudley fumed, his memory going back to the trivialities of the day prior, "as if I had not told you a hundred times over, the proper path leads round about to Millersville and not on this poor road that now directs us across the grassy mount yonder."

"Be that as it may," responded his companion, "the battle is before us now, and there is no turning back, though it may be seemly for you to think otherwise."

Dudley was not finished with his complaints. "Were it not for my goodly steed having been stolen in the night, we would be in the battle now as we speak!"

"Ah, yes, your goodly steed," said O'Reilly, reflectively, pausing by a tuft of grass. "Well, truth be told, I loaned him to a passing knight for a small token of silver when you were asleep."

"You!" Dudley's voice and visage were now all full of wrath. "You sold my fair Philip!"

"Nay, loaned," corrected the other, ignoring the rage and plodding on. "The knight had greater need than you or I at the time, and when we reach the other side of this fine field, and supposing that neither knight nor horse has yet perished, you shall have your fair Philip back again."

"Well, scurvy lad!" burst out Dudley, "Explain this treason! How a passing knight might have better need than I at such a time!"

Ignoring the slight, O'Reilly continued, "It is easy to explain. You had not yet made your mind up whether or not we would continue on toward the battle here in Dunshire or go far north past Millersville and circle round to Sothersbane. Indeed, you spoke of an oath to support our brothers traveling north, while I heard you tell our excellent companions that you would carry me hence, so verily, when the fine Knight Wesley came requesting assistance and we had naught else to offer, I loaned him your animal for a goodly sum."

"Knight Wesley," Dudley repeated thoughtfully, his attitude somewhat diminished. "Well, then, perhaps you did not do so poorly, after all, for he is as fine and faithful a man I have ever known, but you have still treated me in a deceptive fashion."

"I?" O'Reilly now sounded incredulous. "Treated you in a deceptive fashion? Howbeit?"

"Why did you not directly tell me the whole tale instead of forcing me to awake to such poor news?" Dudley demanded.

"You were asleep in the tent after drinking yourself into a stupor, and in the early morning hours, you were in such a rage by the misunderstanding that I betook myself apart until you had cooled your heels. And now, the opportunity has finally presented itself to speak, and so I speak and have spoken thusly."

Seeing the reasoning of his companion, Dudley simply muttered for a bit under his breath as they plodded on. Finally, he said, "You did fair, man, but simply fair and not as a true man would do to his brother."

"Then I did wrongly," O'Reilly said, suddenly showing impatience with an unexpected hint of mockery, "but I freely admit my own fault, for I am unable to act as a true man, for I am no man."

"You are no man," Dudley replied in a similar vein with mockery and repugnance, glancing at his companion with an oath. "Explain yourself, then, you devilish fellow."

"I mean what I say, for I am no man." O'Reilly stopped at this juncture and began to unbuckle the chinstrap of the helmet. "I intended to keep my face a full secret, as my fellows charged me, but you are such an impertinent rascal that I am willing to break my word and show you the truth that I am no man."

"Of a certain?" Dudley said, now incredulous, seeing the helmet come off and an un-bearded face with long hair appear.

"Aye," O'Reilly confirmed, revealing the face of a young and fair-faced lady. "Now you see me plainly?"

"Aye," Dudley echoed, baffled. "No man, indeed."

"And now, shall we put aside this scurvy argument and go on hence to meet our brothers who are already in the heat of the battle?" Not waiting for an answer, O'Reilly turned to go, helmet swinging from her hand.

"O, but stay a bit," Dudley called out, his thoughts all in a muddle.

O'Reilly paused in step and glanced back.

Approaching her, he extended his gloved hand. "I was but a fool to think otherwise, for I knew you not but as a common knight. How came it to be that you are no man, but a woman?"

"I have always been as such," O'Reilly said calmly, though she was inclined to laugh merrily at the interchange. "You may have heard of me as the Lady Abigail of Westwood, disguised as Knight John O'Reilly to protect my fellows, but it matters not, for they have safely arrived and performed their quest, and I shall be reunited with them within the hour."

Cursing himself, Dudley struck his thigh with his glove and then said in his most courteous manner, "Ah, but had the Lady Abigail invited me into her confidence from the beginning—"

"Nay," she interrupted, "for you made it quite clear that you never intended to inquire after me in any way. You only desired to speak of your own self and of your own doings."

"Ah, but how wrong it was of me!" Dudley cried out with sudden emotion.

Seeing her companion's changed face, she shook her head and steeled her composure. "Say no more, friend knight. The matter is forgiven. Let us not waste any more precious time but go hence immediately."

"No, but stay," Dudley said, his voice now cajoling. "I have but a few words more to speak to you."

At that, Lady Abigail appeared twice as determined to go and put her back to him. "Come along, friend knight. Let us neither be childish nor hasty in our words at this present time."

"Childish! Hasty!" he cried, hurrying after her. "There is nothing further from my mind, but it is a true and noble thought that has occurred to me."

Sighing with impatience, she turned and looked upon her companion. "Pray now, what is so noble a thought as to keep us from the great duty that lies ahead?"

"Marry me!" Dudley pronounced quickly, throwing himself upon one knee in the grassy field. "It was good and kind providence that threw our paths together, and now there is no doubt in my mind what a bonny life we shall live hereafter!"

Lady Abigail stood still in bewilderment for a moment and then shook her head resolutely. "Friend," she said calmly, "there is a time and place for marriage, and neither time nor place is with us presently. Our time and place is defending our brothers for our king, and we are stalling."

Sounding overly desperate, Dudley said, "Then promise me the honor of marrying me after the battle!"

"No, indeed," Lady Abigail replied as gently as she knew how, "no such promises can be made, for nothing has changed in either of our circumstances to warrant such a life-altering decision."

Dudley rose upon his feet at this juncture and stared at her. "Nothing has changed? Nothing could warrant such a life-altering decision? How can you speak in such a beastly way toward me? Have you not a single kind thought toward the grand institution of marriage?"

"I have many a kind thought," the Lady responded, still patient, "but again, there is a time and place for such a calling, and our present calling does not intersect with such a one as that."

"O, stubborn woman!" Dudley cried out in distraction, turning away and throwing up his arms as if appealing to the heavens. Pacing about, he said, "How can I make you understand that I adore you and that such a life as ours together would be bliss indeed?"

"And how can I make you understand that you are acting the common fool with blinders preventing you from seeing the truth that is before us?" the noblewoman countered, her voice remaining calm and steady but her inner rage growing. "For the last time, shall we go together toward the battle, or shall I go on alone and rejoin our brothers while you blather on as an idiot?"

"Common fool?" Dudley repeated in shock. "Blather on as an idiot? What intolerant language! I will not suffer it to be spoken in my presence anymore!"

"Very well," Lady Abigail concluded, looking down at the helmet in her hand. "Then I shall leave your presence and follow those who have a better understanding of our duties toward the adventure that is before us."

"O, woe is me," Dudley muttered under his breath. "Curse my misery."

"Do not fear," she replied, looking up at him steadily. "I shall not torture you any longer." Reaching into her side pockets, Lady Abigail went on. "The money I carry is mostly yours because of your horse Philip, and only a small portion is mine, but you may have it all in thanks for your kindness and generosity along the journey. Likewise, you shall keep this beast as a token of my goodwill and forgiveness of your uncouth behavior. And so," she said, handing over the money pouch along with the reins to her horse, "I thank you."

Dudley watched with his mouth open as she turned to walk away. He glanced from the money pouch in one hand to the horse's reins in his other and then gazed after her departing figure.

"Is there no way I can convince you otherwise?" he shouted. "Must we part like enemies after all this time?"

Lady Abigail walked on, affixing her helmet once more and straightening her sword in her belt. She acted heedless of his words but heard him quite clearly for some time.

Another five yards and Dudley cried out, "O, curse my misery! Curses upon the false impressions I had toward you at the very first!"

Another ten yards and Dudley became completely unglued. "Vile wench!" he screamed after her in a vile rage. "After everything I did for you! Ungrateful witch!"

So, leaving that miserable and preposterous knight with his untimely proposal, the great lady walked on, following her calling to support her brothers in battle. Undistracted by the promised comforts and pleasant addictions of life, she braced herself for the upcoming difficulty with hopes of reaching the other side in happiness and peace.

Meanwhile, our shameful Knight Dudley found it needful to collect his bearings after issuing his ungainly proposal. The poor fellow was so plagued by unpleasant thoughts and emotions that he was uncertain whether to head into battle or take another course of action. Such was the life of a man driven by fits, rages, whims, and fancies.

Happily, the ungallant Dudley recovered after a short space of time when another romantic thought came into his fair head. Mounting the Lady Abigail's horse with sudden urgency, the distracted fellow wheeled about and charged across the field toward the rising sun, determined to find himself a new measure of glory with which to assuage his battered emotions.

CHAPTER FOUR

An Italian Love Story

PART ONE

There once was a man named Luigi Bertolli who lived in a great big house with his very large family. Besides himself, there was his Papa, his Mamma, his very old Grandmamma, his younger brother Filippo, Filippo's wife Anabella, and the three little girls, Marguerite, Lilianna, and Contessa. Plus, a great number of uncles, aunts, and cousins often came and went as they pleased.

Luigi, as the eldest son, stood in line to inherit the family villa, but he disappointed his beloved father because he did not care about temporal riches. Luigi preferred to study at his little desk in the large library, work in the fields with the common laborers, and serve in the neighboring towns with the local priest.

"What is wrong with you?" Papa shouted at his son when he reached his thirtieth year. Luigi had just returned from a trip with the priest, worn out and tired from all the work they had done among the poor. "You worthless good-for-nothing! I give the villa to Filippo instead!"

"Do not be angry, Papa," Luigi had said quietly. "I love God's people."

Then Papa's wrath subsided as he embraced his tired son, sending him to bed with a couple of manservants to care for him.

One spring, Mamma had a visit from two of her second cousins who brought along a fine rich man named Geraldo Guiseppe di Constanzo. Signore di Constanzo was very impressed by the villa with all of its beautiful trees, sprawling gardens, and prosperous fields outside and all of its high ceilings, ornate woodwork, and spacious rooms inside. He was especially enamored by the three pretty little granddaughters, Marguerite, Lilianna, and Contessa, who were very happy little girls and loved to dance and sing.

"Ah, you must hire a good teacher for their letters," he told Mamma, "They must stay here and be happy and sing and never leave! The world is a terrible place." Then Geraldo went on to speak of several young women he was acquainted with who were very cultured and intelligent and would do an excellent job tutoring.

Papa immediately began to argue that he planned to hire the same man who had taught Luigi and Filippo, but Geraldo just laughed. He pointed to Luigi, then to Filippo, and then to the little girls, and he shook his head.

"You cannot bring in an ugly old man to teach such delicate flowers! They will lose their song and their dance. I will send you a fine young lady at once."

And so, it was decided. Within a week, Geraldo sent his niece, a young lady named Regina Zambino, to work at the villa. She was quiet, intelligent, pretty, and had none of her sponsor's obtrusive mannerisms. As Filippo and Anabella did not want the girls to start their schooling until the summer was over, Regina began working primarily by cooking and cleaning in exchange for her room and board, but she also became acquainted with the little girls and grew to love them very much.

During the day, the villa was a very busy and noisy place except for the afternoon rest hour. In the evening, the family and activities settled down, and Regina found many enjoyable things to do during that quiet time of day. Sometimes Regina liked exploring the big rambling house or walking around the gardens and hayfields, but most of the time, she preferred to sit quietly in the big library or under a tree outside and read a book.

It was on one such evening that Regina met Luigi. He had been on another trip with the village priest for some days and was riding back on his horse, but a servant had relieved him of his animal and his belongings by the barns. Luigi decided to walk back up to the great house alone and enjoy the beauty of the quiet evening before finding some supper and retiring for the night.

Regina sat peacefully beneath the big elm tree facing west toward the setting sun when Luigi came around the bend in the path to the house. He stood there for a moment, feeling unusually curious to know what she was reading. When he continued to walk closer, Regina glanced up and noticed him.

"Hello," he said and then asked what she was reading.

At that, she blushed and explained shyly that she found St. Austin's *Meditations* most favorable for such a lovely evening.

Luigi smiled, the dried dust cracking on his tired face. It was a book that was dear to his own heart. "Most favorable indeed," he echoed, and then, turning to look at the setting sun, he began to quote a passage from memory about the glory of God and the goodness of rest for His beloved servants.

Regina rose as he spoke, awed by the devotion in his tone that demonstrated his love for God and His creation. But when Luigi turned toward her again, Papa's voice came booming from the courtyard, sending several servants streaming out across the lawn toward them, gabbling in excitement that Master Luigi had returned to his villa.

Upon hearing such news, Regina felt awkward and nervously curtseyed to Luigi before quietly withdrawing so that he might be welcomed home properly by his father and servants without distraction.

In the following weeks, Luigi rarely had the opportunity to see or speak to Regina except in mixed company, but she often considered how kind and respectful he was toward her in their brief interactions. His behavior was so unlike the arrogant attitudes of the rest of the household that she wondered what would happen if he were to speak to her plainly about his feelings. As custom did not permit such direct and open conversation on the topic, the summer passed by without incident.

Part Two

In the first month of fall, on the week just before the busiest harvest season, Papa, Mamma, and Grandmamma went on holiday to visit distant cousins in the city. On the third morning of their absence, an unexpected commotion occurred at the house.

Anabella flew downstairs in a passionate fit, waving an open letter in her hand and declaring to Filippo that she loved another man. Dismissing everyone with a sharp flick of her wrist, she left the house with nothing but a carpetbag containing her most prized possessions.

In an instant, the house was thrown into chaos. After filling the house with curses and shouts, Filippo retired to his room in a dreadful state of shock and began to weep inconsolably.

Meanwhile, the little girls wept loudly for their mamma, and the nannies attempted to comfort the little ones while their own shocked tears streamed down their faces. The maids and cooks hurried about, spreading more gossip and rumors, and the manservants rushed out to the fields to call Luigi in from his work.

In the midst of it, Regina stood still in the middle of the great hall by the ornate banister, not sure what she should do.

Luigi came in from the fields, besmeared with dirt and smelling of cattle. He ordered the servants to continue their work as unto the Lord without permitting idle chatter to multiply among them. He found the nannies in the yard with the little girls, whose tempers had been somewhat abated, and left them to go address his brother. He found Regina standing on the bottom step, gazing up the stairs and listening to the wails of Filippo issuing from his bedroom.

She turned and looked at Luigi, her dark eyes expressive, but she said nothing.

Luigi gave her a grim smile and then paused, reaching into his shirt to take out a small wooden cross he kept tied around his neck with a rough strap of leather. He pulled it free and gently pressed it into her hand, admonishing her to pray for the comfort of his stricken brother. Then, he went up the stairs without another word.

Regina watched him go, admiring his bravery and courage in such a trying time, and then she slipped out of doors to walk around the villa and pray quietly and steadily for the rest of the morning.

At the end of several very long and trying days, a footman found Luigi in the library and passed him a message. His parents had received his letter, in which he had informed them of the tragedy, and they would be returning the following afternoon. Nodding wearily to the deliverer, Luigi thanked and dismissed him, turning back to his desk to write another sheet of paper.

An hour later, at nearly eleven o'clock, Regina found Luigi dozing on the couch nearest his desk, exhaustion written all over his face.

"Master Luigi, you must find time to sleep," she said to him quietly, standing in the middle of the room with a candle in her hand.

Luigi rose wearily and stood there, gazing at her.

She hesitated from leaving, wondering what he would say, even though she also felt that it was improper for them to be alone in the same room.

"The Bertolli villa will not be home to you forever," he said quietly and unexpectedly, turning back to his desk to pick up his own candle.

Regina felt a sudden stab of grief as a thousand fears leaped to her mind. Was she not good enough in her work here? Did he no longer care for her? Was he privy to some knowledge about the sudden change in his brother Filippo's life that would uproot her from her happy existence at the villa?

"What do you mean?" she wondered, hardly able to think straight.

At that, he sighed wearily and shook his head. Motioning her out of the room ahead of him, he followed her out of the library and closed the door behind them, bidding her a good night as they went their separate ways in the dark house.

In the weeks that followed, the household began to settle into another kind of rhythm, but Regina's mind still buzzed with unanswered questions. Life had changed dramatically for everyone, but she saw no reason to leave the villa. She secretly admitted to herself that she loved Luigi, and in fact, she loved him even more in the middle of the family's trials. She accepted the simple fact that all of their futures were as uncertain and tenuous as Filippo's happiness, but Luigi's phrase echoed in her mind, and she wondered when it would be that she would be forced to depart from the villa against her will.

Then one day, a particular maid who openly disdained Regina came into the room where Regina was teaching letters to Marguerite and Lilianna. Regina looked up at her in surprise, but went right on teaching until the time was up, and then she dismissed the little girls to their nannies.

The maid had been waiting patiently the whole while and eyeing Regina now and again in a certain malicious way as she pretended to dust the room. Seeing that the young charges were leaving, the maid smiled a bit viciously and sauntered over to where Regina was setting her papers and books back in order and cleaning off the little slates.

"Your uncle Geraldo was here," Sara began, a sneer developing on her face.

Regina looked up in alarm. On the one hand, she had no cause for fear, for Uncle Geraldo had introduced her to the Bertollis in the first place. But at the same time, Regina knew that she was at the constant beck and call of her uncle, for Uncle Geraldo had long arranged with her parents that the son of his faithful manager would marry her after completing his studies.

To her knowledge, that man still had two years left in studies, but as brilliant as he was, Tomaso Pasquale Giovanni was also a very sickly fellow. Every summer since she was five years old, Regina had seen Tomaso during a brief visit so that they might be better acquainted with each other before their approaching marriage. The past three years that she had seen him, Tomaso had been so ill that he had not said a word to her, and he was constantly in need of doctors and private tutors to assist him at his luxurious home so that he need not go outside.

Though she had never admitted it to anyone, Regina hated visiting Tomaso. It was not that Regina hated Tomaso, for she actually felt sorry for him, but she hated how it was that he had never been allowed to fend for himself, enjoy the great world, and spend time outside in the sunshine. He was pale, sickly, and worrisome, and sometimes Regina wondered if Tomaso was afraid of marrying her as much as she was afraid of being married to him. She had secretly resigned herself to her fate at the age of twelve and then resolved that she would be kind to him and try to make him healthier, but if he died, she would become a nun.

All of that suddenly flashed through Regina's mind, as if a distant dream was returning to haunt her, and then she looked up to see Sara laughing in a rather nasty way. She thought again of Uncle Geraldo and took a deep breath, forcing the worry to fade from her expression.

The maid was prattling on. "He left you a letter. He said that he has a most urgent matter to inform you about and that he would be back next week or shortly thereafter."

"Thank you, Sara," Regina said politely and rose with all of her teaching materials, quickly sweeping out of the room before the maid could say anything further.

After putting away the books and papers, Regina retreated to her room, where she found the letter sitting neatly on the big dresser by the doorway. She closed and locked the door before reaching for the letter, breaking the seal and tearing the envelope open with trembling fingers to read as follows:

My dear Gina,

Our unfortunate Tomaso, beloved of my soul, and no less beloved to you as betrothed to him, is faring no better this season than he was in the last. We have determined to send him to the seacoast for a much-needed rest. He is setting out promptly on the 5th of next month for three fortnights of rest.

Tomaso has requested that you join him for the second week of his stay and remain with him for at least half of the allotted time. He will have all of the necessary doctors and nurses attending to him and needs not your particular care, but your emotional support will be deemed greatly helpful to his recovery.

I will send for you as soon as he has gone so you have adequate time to prepare to join him.

I remain,

Your affectionate Uncle,

Geraldo Giuseppe di Costanzo

Regina sat down upon her bed after reading the short message, letting out a great and weary sigh, but then hastily rose to hide the letter among her belongings in such a way that she was certain the maids would be unable to find it. Then she immediately went outside, the wooden cross clasped in her right palm, and began to walk through a recently mowed field of wheat, wondering what she could do and praying that she would do the right thing.

Later at supper, Regina learned that Papa Bertolli had also received a message from Uncle Geraldo. After all, her uncle had made it publicly known that he would be sending two young women to replace Regina as the girls' tutor at the villa by the following week. There was, then, no need for her to tremble or hide her dreadful news, for the whole household knew about it.

What did Luigi think?

Regina could only wonder, for she did not see him at supper or that evening in the library, though she waited until nearly ten o'clock to see if he would appear. The next morning, she arose early to see him before he left for the fields, but he was nowhere to be found.

It was only through the compassionate maid Bettina that Regina discovered that when Luigi first heard of the news, he had immediately packed his bags and begged his father to allow him to go help Brother Andre in a neighboring villa with a great need that had suddenly arisen.

Despite the story she had been told, Regina was certain that Luigi had left because of her. She felt a great tearing in her heart along with grief that could not be measured, certain that she had caused him pain, even though she had no control over the situation herself.

Every night for a week, she went into the library long after the household had gone to sleep to sit down at Luigi's desk and light a flickering candle. She always picked up a quill and paper to write to him, but every night, she set them aside in despair, unable to put into words what she felt in her heart.

PART THREE

The following Tuesday, two women showed up, her replacements in teaching the children. Put out of that job and having few belongings to pack or prepare, Regina spent most of her days wandering through the fields and gardens, wishing that she could help bring in the harvest or that she had something else profitable to do before her uncle Geraldo arrived to take her to the seashore to be with Tomaso.

And, still, Luigi stayed away from home. Alone in her grief and desperation, Regina found herself unable to eat and unable to sleep. Every day, she went through the house, trying to be helpful but always seeing the eyes of the hateful Sara upon her, always hearing the whispers from the gossips, always feeling from the other two women teachers that she no longer had a place at the villa. Every night, she lay in her bed, staring out the window at the night sky, her fingers clutching the wooden cross that Luigi had given her, unable to find the strength to draw the curtains and close her eyes in rest.

That Friday night, Regina lay awake as usual, considering how it was that in a few short days, she would be gone from the villa forever. Uncle Geraldo had originally planned to come for her that morning, but he had been delayed and requested that Papa Bertolli send her things in a cart following the family as they went to Sunday worship so that he could meet them all at the church for Mass.

Regina thought of Luigi, for he was never far from her mind, and how he had prophetically said that she would not stay forever at the villa. Had he known, then, of everything that was to come to pass? And if so, why had he not explained it to her himself to better prepare her for the sudden change?

Rising in desperation, Regina wrapped her shawl about her shoulders and left her room in her nightgown and bare feet without a candle, clutching the wooden cross and carefully making her way through the dark house by the light of the moon slipping in through the windows.

When she reached the first floor and stood in the great hallway, she considered going out into the gardens but heard the front door turning on its hinges as someone entered the foyer. As the sound of boots upon the hardwood floor came toward her, Regina shrank into the shadows. She watched silently as the figure paused in the hallway where she had just been standing and bent down to remove his boots. A gleam of moonshine struck his face as he stood upright again, and she knew it was him.

"Luigi," she whispered and flew from her corner toward him.

He dropped his boots and turned toward her, amazement flitting across his features. "Gina," he said, clinging to her desperately, weariness and relief mixed in his voice.

They heard the sound of footsteps coming from another part of the house and quickly withdrew into the shadows.

"I thought you had left. I thought you were to be wed," Luigi's voice murmured in her ear as he still held her tightly in his arms.

Regina drew back and looked up at him, the desperation as thick in her voice as the tears she attempted to restrain. "It is against my will. I do not love him. My uncle betrothed me to him when I was a child."

Luigi drew her to his chest again and she stifled the tears as best she could while the footsteps from the back of the house continued approaching. As the dancing shadows of a candle preceded the servant who was slowly entering the hall, the lovers knew that all would be seen in a short minute.

Luigi quickly grabbed Regina's hand and they quietly ran, he in his socked feet and she in her bare ones, all the way up to the top of the stairs. He stopped at the very top step and let go of her hand.

"Go," Luigi whispered to her, nearly pushing her down the hall toward her bedroom. Then he suddenly pulled her back to him and kissed her. "Go," he repeated, pushing her away again. "We will talk tomorrow. Peace be with you."

Regina obediently flew down the hallway to her room, hearing Luigi going back down the stairs to pick up his discarded boots and greet the bleary-eyed servant who stood in the middle of the great hall with a candlestick in hand. Safely in her room, Regina sank into bed again, still clutching the cross, and sighed with relief at their escape from the near discovery. She felt overcome with sudden exhaustion and almost immediately fell asleep.

The morning dawned late upon Regina with the face of Bettina peering down at her with some initial concern, but then smiling to see that the young woman had actually slept through the night. Regina was filled with a sense of urgency as soon as she awoke and quickly rose to prepare for the day, forgoing the tea that Bettina had brought her and simply taking a biscuit and a piece of fruit before going outside.

Regina was certain that she would find Luigi outside in the fields, but he was actually sitting in the courtyard, telling fanciful stories about the big world to his youngest niece while her nanny tittered in the background. Regina watched them for a moment, just out of sight, and then quietly went for a walk around the gardens, gazing at all of the pretty summer flowers that were approaching their last days and would soon be replaced by the fall colors.

Luigi found her standing in a grove of fruit trees some time later and smiled at her when she turned at the sound of his footsteps.

Faced by him in the daylight, Regina felt awkward and at a loss for words, so she said nothing.

Presently, he motioned to her and they began to quietly walk around the gardens together, leaving a bit of distance between each other for the sake of propriety.

Then Luigi asked, curiosity in his tone, "What did you write to me while I was away?"

Regina's eyes quickly went to his face and then dropped to the ground. Flustered, she admitted, "I—I didn't—I never finished anything. I couldn't figure out what to write." Then she looked at him again. "How did you know?"

He smiled slightly. "I saw my name and a couple of words on the blotting pad that were not in my hand, but I could not find any corresponding paper to go with it."

Regina sighed silently, relieved. "I threw all the scraps in the fire. I guess I forgot about the blotting pad."

Without warning, Luigi changed the subject. "Do you wish me to speak to your uncle?"

Regina looked at him in amazement, but then fear quickly passed over her features as she spoke quickly and passionately. "No, please, do not speak to him. Uncle Geraldo is a dangerous man. He is very generous, but he is very controlling, and I fear for anyone who crosses him or suggests something that he does not approve of. He is very stubborn. He will never change his mind."

Luigi stopped by a rosebush whose flowers had long been spent. Fingering a dried petal and lightly touching a thorn-laden stem, he then looked at Regina, seeing her flushed face and clutched hands.

"Please, Master Luigi, I beg you," she said to him nervously, fearing the bold look in his eyes.

Plucking a rosebud that had not yet bloomed, Luigi turned to hand it carefully to her so that she would not be pricked by the thorns. "Do not be afraid," he said quietly,

"I will respect your wishes." And then, "But what will you do?"

"I do not know," she said sadly, "I wish I could go far away from here, away from Uncle Geraldo, away from Tomaso, away from everyone. I would be a nun and serve the poor," she added in a low voice, almost ashamed to admit it.

At that, he smiled a bit and continued to walk around the garden. Regina followed at a bit of a distance, controlling her emotions as she gazed down at the poor little rosebud, feeling a bit similar to it in the way the petals were shut up in its leaves and could only offer thorns to the world.

When they reached the main path to the villa again, Luigi seemed suddenly impatient and distant, as if he had important business on his mind. "I will arrange a journey for you," he said suddenly, turning back to face her. "Look for a boat on the river this evening after supper. Only take your most essential belongings." He stepped away from her, his hands shoved deep in his pockets as he receded into his own thoughts again.

"May God's peace be with you," he threw over his shoulder to her before walking away and disappearing from view.

Regina stood still for a while longer, her thoughts thrown into confusion instead of the peace that Luigi had wished upon her. She imagined that he would be back at his little writing desk for a time, but she was not sure what he meant by looking out for a boat. She knew there was a steady stream at the back of the property but did not know if it led to a nearby river. Either way, she was certain that she did not know how to navigate on the water alone and hoped that he would be there to help her escape.

Her mind muddled from loss of sleep for the last several days, Regina slowly headed back to the villa. Roused by the sound of galloping hooves, she looked up to see a horse and rider quickly departing through the front gate of the villa.

She knew it was him and could only wonder where he was going. Sighing deeply, Regina made her way back to her room, deciding to repack her essentials so she only needed to carry a small bag.

That evening, Regina was not surprised that Luigi was absent from dinner. She had wished to say farewell to him, but then she wondered again if he planned to meet her at the boat. She waited until the sun began to cast long shadows across the gardens and then quietly slipped away with her little bag over her shoulder.

The family was in the living room when she left, happy and chattering with one another. The servants were busily preparing the afternoon meal for the following day. She felt a pang, not being able to bid anyone farewell, but especially not being able to say a word to Bettina, who had watched her with a bit of a sad smile all during dinner as if she knew that something was about to change.

Regina thought about all of this as she slipped in and out of the trees down past the gardens and toward the stream that lay in the woods beyond the furthest fields. She soon came to a little bank and carefully stepped down to the rocks below, seeing a small boat several hundred feet up the stream from where she was standing.

Feeling nervous, she looked all around, up and down the banks of the stream while wondering if Luigi was anywhere in sight. Not seeing him, she approached the little boat tentatively as the darkening shadows continued to creep upon her. Finding the boat small but sturdy, she untied it from a small tree and carefully stepped into the bottom. Her heart pounding with uncertainty, Regina carefully used a single oar to push off the bank, directing the boat into the calm water that gently flowed around a sweeping bend surrounded by overhanging trees.

As the water began to carry her vessel further from the bank, Regina felt a pang, realizing that Luigi was willing for them to be parted for God's work. Not only that, he had actually provided the way for her to leave him forever.

"Farewell, Luigi," she whispered with tears in her eyes as she dipped the oar into the water once more and steered the little boat around the approaching curve in the stream.

Regina's boat took her along quietly for quite some time, and then the large trees and bushes on both sides of the bank began to thin out and become farther and farther apart. In the dimming light, Regina noticed how the small ripples were turning into little waves, and she could sense that the quiet stream would soon turn into a large and rushing river.

Feeling even more nervous, she lifted her oar, not knowing whether to turn aside to the shore or continue ahead.

Just then, Regina heard a voice calling somewhere from her right.

Looking toward the far bank and into the darkening forest, Regina thought she saw a lone shadow standing by the water's edge.

"Hello!" the woman called again.

"Hello," Regina returned shyly, struggling to steer the small craft toward the opposite shore. She reached the edge of the bank just as it became too dark to see anything clearly.

The unknown woman soon reappeared with a torch held high, stepping down the bank toward her. "I am Sister Antoinette. Are you Sister Regina?"

"Yes," Regina said, feeling just as shy as before, "but I have not taken my vows yet."

"But you are still a sister," the woman said kindly, taking the rope and helping her out of the boat. "Come, we have been waiting for you."

Regina watched the woman deftly tie the rope to a tree along the riverbank and then followed her by torchlight through the woods until she could see a small clearing and a lean-to with an inviting fire burning in front of it.

Several other women were sitting around the fire and rose to welcome Regina. They were all very kind and gener-ous, recognizing that she was tired from her evening journey and encouraging her to make herself comfortable for the night.

"We have a long journey tomorrow, as well as the day after," Sister Antoinette told her, helping her settle down in a roughly-made sack under the lean-to. "Do get some sleep, Sister Regina, and we will see you in the morning." Making the sign of the cross above them both, the woman gently lifted Regina's hand and kissed it before rejoining her sisters around the fire as they talked in a low voice about the mission they were on.

Regina felt as if she was in a daze as she lay there, allowing the night sounds to lull her to sleep. She clutched the little wooden cross in her hand as she prayed the Our Father and thanked the Lord that Luigi had helped her escape. Yet, her prayers were not without tears as she wondered if she would ever see her love again.

Part Four

Regina and the sisters traveled south to help a village of refugees who were quarantined from the rest of the people in the surrounding towns and cities. They spent several weeks in a cramped and crowded place that was hidden from the rest of the world, relieving the sick and helping the strong find meaning and purpose in life.

As the colder months approached and that particular mission appeared to be nearing its end, the sisters invited Regina to journey north with them to their convent in the city of Luciana. Sister Antoinette specifically encouraged her to join the sisters by taking her vows and permanently becoming one of them.

Regina considered her options each day as they traveled north. She often woke with a start in the middle of the night and lay there quietly, waiting for sleep to return while praying for help and guidance. She was tossed and turned in her thoughts and did not know the way to go, but still, she waited, prayed, and sought an answer while continuing along the journey.

The evening that the sisters returned to the Convent of Santa Maria della Vittoria in the city of Luciana, Regina met Mother Bianca, a very kind and generous woman with wise eyes and a mysterious smile.

"You are very welcome here, Sister Regina," Mother Bianca told the young woman. "Sister Antoinette has told me of your diligence and fortitude in the mission. We look forward to having you serve as one of us."

Regina responded politely and was happy to retire alone in her humble quarters in the big castle. She stood by the tall window in the small room, pulling back one of the drapes that overlooked the courtyard. She could faintly see the city beyond, little lights gleaming from the top of lampposts, and wondered if the decision that she had been trying to reach had already been made for her.

Regina slept well that night but woke up very early before the morning Mass. She decided to take a walk around the convent while she still had her freedom, and soon her steps took her out of the gates of the convent and into the city of Luciana.

Regina wandered up and down the streets as the merchants began to put out their wares and people began to go about their business for the day. Coming upon a small group of children, she caught a glimpse of little girls in white dresses with their curly hair, rosy cheeks, laughing mouths, and big brown eyes. Immediately, she felt a pang, thinking about the three little girls, Marguerite, Lilianna, and Contessa. Then she began to think about Luigi, and tears came to her eyes as she stood stock still in the middle of the walkway until a group of boys with a couple of excited stray dogs almost knocked her down.

Hiding against the nearest building until the whooping and hollering passed her by, Regina turned and looked back at the convent from which she came. How could she take her vows if she still loved Luigi and the children? She stood in indecision for a time and then turned and began walking away from the convent, going deeper and deeper into the city.

Without warning, Regina was suddenly caught up in a swarm of people who were happily chattering and hurrying to get somewhere. She felt dread steal over her, not knowing where she was going. After only a couple of minutes, the group finally stopped and Regina found herself in the city square, listening to a speaker vigorously talking about his grand new plan to reform city politics.

Not interested in the speech, Regina began to carefully ease her way out of the crowd and decided to return to the convent for morning Mass. As she began to head back up the same street the large crowd had just brought her down, she suddenly noticed that a man leaning against one of the nearby city buildings was staring at her while blowing smoke from a cigar.

Regina suddenly shuddered, recognizing the man as Marco Stanzone, one of her uncle's henchmen who constantly roamed the land to spy on family and friends and make sure they were doing what they were supposed to be doing. Not only was he dangerous and a villain toward all people who crossed her uncle, but Marco Stanzone was also a greedy and lecherous fellow that no decent woman could feel safe around.

Feeling dread and fear steal over her, Regina wondered if it would be worth running as fast as she could to claim sanctuary in Santa Maria. Before she could find a clear path out of the city, however, Marco was in front of her, looking down his long hooked nose with his beady eyes shadowed by bushy eyebrows.

"Hello, Signore Stanzone," Regina said calmly, folding her hands in front of her chest and forcing herself to act serenely.

He grinned unpleasantly, showing gaps in his teeth from long years of tobacco usage and poor eating habits. "What are you doing here, Miss Zambino? Your uncle Geraldo has been looking for you everywhere."

"Poor uncle!" Regina said, her face flushing bright pink as she feigned surprise. "I sent him a letter that I was on a journey to help the sisters serve the poor. Why didn't he write back to me?"

At that, Marco scratched his head slightly, not realizing that Regina's blushing face was a result of her telling him a series of direct lies. Then he shrugged. "Maybe he did not know where to write. Where are you staying?"

"At the Convent of Santa Maria, right here," Regina replied, her face returning to its normal color now that she was telling the truth. "We just returned from a trip and they want me to take my vows. Will Uncle come for the ceremony?"

Marco seemed further puzzled by that. "What about Tomaso?" he wondered, leering in an evil way.

"Oh, Tomaso," Regina said, suddenly appearing sad. "Poor Tomaso. How is he doing?"

At that, Marco seemed uninterested. "Oh, same as always." He shrugged and then motioned up the street toward the convent. "It is dangerous for a pretty girl like you to be wandering around this early in the morning," he said in a crafty tone. "I will walk you back."

"Thank you, Signore," Regina said, doing her best to act grateful while a horrible fear settled into her stomach.

She walked on ahead of him at his insistence, keeping up a steady pace and navigating the path with the most people possible, forcing herself to remain silent and calm, no matter how his heavy breathing behind her made her want to break into a run and scream for help. She sent up a continuous stream of prayers the whole walk until they finally reached the convent. Greatly relieved, Regina gave Marco a tiny wave as she slipped back in through the gate and headed to her room to change before morning Mass.

After that morning, Regina was in constant dread of leaving the convent, fearing she would see Marco Stanzone at every corner of the street. Even when she went out with the sisters as a group, she hid next to the largest of them, not wanting to be seen by the big swarthy fellow.

Then, one day, just as the sisters were returning to the convent from the market, Marco approached them, his hand extended toward Regina. The nuns looked at him with a bit of fearful suspicion but parted ways and allowed him to approach her.

"A letter from your uncle Geraldo Giuseppe di Costanzo," he said in a formal tone, bowing slightly and causing a lock of greasy hair to fall over his eyes momentarily. Straightening, he grinned unpleasantly, handed her the letter, and then disappeared into a dark alley to watch her and the sisters pass through the gate into the convent courtyard.

Regina avoided the stares and questions of the sisters and took the letter up to her room before opening it. It was written in her uncle's usual messy and hurried handwriting and read as follows:

My dearest Gina,

Had I known of your wish and desire to join the Convent of Santa Maria della Vittoria from the beginning, I would have hastily done my best to encourage you in that calling from our most gracious God, our forever blessed Savior, and our lovely and immaculate Lady, whom you have always resembled in your simple beauty and chaste attitude.

O my poor and deluded child, there is a better convent in which to take your vows that is much closer to home, so I must command you not to commit yourself to the

Reverend Mother of that city, blessed as she may be. I have also written to her on this matter, recommending that she speak with the Reverend Mother Angelica of Naples if she finds it necessary to do so.

As for our beloved Tomaso, whom I am assured you are fearful of offending as much as I was affrighted to bring him news of your happy state, do not allow yourself to be saddened any longer. When I referred the matter to his attention, he remained placid and assured me that the calling to holy vows was as blessed a state as one could hope for and that he had even considered them himself at one point or another. He sends you his greetings and well-wishes and assures you that when you return home to speak to him of the betrothal, terms can be reached that are satisfactory to all parties.

I shall send for you after the winter season, so be at peace at the convent as you live among the devoted sisters and look for me in early spring.

I remain,

Your affectionately devoted Uncle,

Geraldo Giuseppe di Costanzo

Knowing that there was no cause for her to hide the letter, Regina tucked it into her dress and went to afternoon Mass with the sisters.

Afterward, she went directly upstairs to Mother Bianca's hallway and stood there patiently for a whole hour until Sister Theresa came out and kindly told her that the Reverend Mother could see her now.

Timidly, Regina went into the big room that was arranged both as an office and as a private prayer chapel, wishing that she had something with which to cover her head instead of standing out among all of the sisters who had long since taken their vows.

Mother Bianca was standing by an ornate cross, her prayer beads in hand, and turned to see the young woman trembling slightly. Smiling reassuringly, the older woman came forward, extending one of her hands graciously and allowing Regina to approach.

"You come about your uncle," she said wisely.

"Oh, Reverend Mother," Regina said passionately, falling on her knees and holding out the letter, the tears suddenly springing to her eyes. "My uncle bids me to be at peace here, but he will not allow me to take my vows, and I do not know whether he means to force me to marry

Tomaso or if he has other plans—he is such an evil and dangerous fellow!"

"Ah, child," Mother Bianca said kindly, taking the letter and setting it aside on her desk as she raised the weeping girl and bid her sit down in a nearby chair. "Let us take this matter to our kind and gracious Savior, who delivers us from all of our enemies and bids our sorrows cease."

Regina listened with rapt attention to the wise woman as she continued to speak about relying upon the loving care of God, mixing her admonitions with fervent prayers, and then bidding Regina to dwell in peace at the convent for the winter.

"And then what will you have me do?" Regina wondered, her countenance cleared but her mind still full of questions.

"Ah, child," Mother Bianca said with a slow smile. "We cannot rush the ways of God. We must allow time and circumstance to pass before we make a decision. Be at peace here and allow the work to draw you closer to our Savior and our blessed Lady, and then we shall talk more after the winter has passed."

Obediently, Regina submitted to those instructions and then left for her own room to pray and consider how she could best keep a peaceful attitude for the next season.

Part Five

As the winter passed by, Regina occupied herself in the simple but busy life at the convent, often feeling as if she could remain at that place for the rest of her life. Once the spring breezes began to warm the air and the daylight began to arrive earlier each morning, however, she felt a strange and unexpected restlessness. She patiently waited for some sort of news, whether from her uncle or Mother Bianca, but the next directive came from an unexpected source.

One day, Sister Antoinette came to her, relating some of the journeys she had completed that winter, for she was hardly ever at the convent.

"Sister Gina," she said afterward, "I have spoken with our gracious Reverend Mother about your situation."

Regina was immediately curious and leaned forward, listening with anticipation.

"It seems to me that since some in your family are still uncomfortable with the idea of you taking holy vows that you remain in a difficult situation right now."

"Yes, but couldn't I take vows even if my uncle does not approve?" Regina wondered. "Do not the holy saints say that to follow God is better than to obey the opinion of man? Did not even Saint Peter and Saint John tell that to the councils who beat them for their obedience to our Savior?"

Sister Antoinette smiled slightly, pleased to hear the simple courage and devotion in Regina's words. "Yes, my sister, but you know that it is greatly discouraged for a young woman to disobey her family in these matters, even if it seems that the family's desires are standing in the way of God."

Regina held her tongue, sensing that Sister Antoinette had some other suggestion to offer.

"And, as you know, it is not proper for guests to remain long at the convent who have not yet taken their vows."

"Yes," Regina agreed, feeling sad that she was still considered a guest according to the definitions and terms of the convent, even though in a practical sense she was as devoted as any of the nuns.

"I have spoken with our gracious Reverend Mother on the matter, and she has permitted me to ask you if you would come with me on the next mission trip."

At that, Regina's heart was lightened, and she looked at Sister Antoinette with joy. "Please, let me come," she said, reaching out and taking her sister's hand in both of hers, foregoing all formality. "I would be blessed to serve wherever we go."

"Then it is settled," Sister Antoinette said with a smile, rising to bless Regina. "I will speak with Sister Diana, who will have more details for me next week, for I believe she is leading the next trip. I will also have Sister Anna let you know when to be ready, and we are greatly blessed to have you serve with us."

Two weeks later, Regina found herself packing up and leaving with a small group of traveling sisters led by Sister Diana of the Sanctuary of Saint Patrick, a true saint who came from the north to teach younger sisters about the life of poverty and sacrifice. Finding the sisters from Santa Maria to be more advanced than her regular charges, Sister Diana decided that they would forgo the regular training and spend most of their time encouraging the believers who relieved the poor in the surrounding cities.

For the following three months, the small group lived as pilgrims, traveling from city to city, meeting other sisters and brothers who worked with the poor, and seeking to bring rest, peace, and encouragement to all they encountered. They also picked up a fair number of other individuals along the way who desired to travel with them, including a widowed woman named Catarina and her two young children.

Regina greatly enjoyed the new assignment that she had been given, not only because she was able to travel, thus satisfying the strange restlessness that she had previously felt toward the end of the winter, but also because the excitement of meeting other sisters and brothers in an effort to bless them.

The arrival of Catarina and her children also brought her great happiness, for she had greatly missed the chance to love children throughout the whole winter. She often found most happiness and contentment in the company of the mother and her children back at camp instead of being out with the other sisters on the busy streets.

The only thing that caused Regina some anxiety was the knowledge that her uncle's henchman, Marco Stanzone, had also joined their motley group of pilgrims. Not directly, of course, for no wicked and villainous person was permitted to associate with the holy group. Yet, Regina knew that he had been following them the whole while, for every once in a while, when they were in the city, she would see a shadowed face and feel a strange and familiar chill.

She often woke with a start in the night and forced herself to pray for safety, not only for herself but also for the whole group. After all, she knew that it was not beyond the realm of possibility for the evil man to attack and kill them all in his effort to gain access to her for whatever nefarious plans her uncle had in store.

Despite that one trial in her days, life continued pleasantly for Regina that whole spring and summer. Regardless of the physical hardships the group faced in traveling and the various dangers they regularly encountered, the company of the sisters continued to grow and strengthen. As Sister Diana often admonished them all, the Lord was guiding their steps, and He would bless them in their efforts as they followed His call.

One week later, the group found themselves in a smaller city surrounded by little towns and villages. Since they were more accustomed to larger cities that were more affected by poverty, some in the group asked Sister Diana why they were going to the relatively obscure city of Speranza, which had one of the lowest crime and poverty rates in the whole district.

As she was prone to, Sister Diana did not offer a direct explanation. Instead, she told the sisters and children around the campfire that it was by the leading of God that they were now approaching the city of Speranza and that it was by trusting in His hope that they would soon learn how to be a blessing to the people in that region as well.

The following day, the sisters broke up into pairs as was their custom while they prepared to go forth for their regular ministry. On this particular morning, Sister Diana asked Regina to accompany her to visit one of the local churches where she had been invited by the priest to come and talk. Since Sister Diana and Sister Anna often were the most regular companions, and since Regina usually went out with Catarina and her children, Regina was a bit surprised by the invitation but willingly went along with Sister Diana.

The two of them met with Father Antonio, a kindly man with a graying beard who spoke to them at length about the blessed state of his parish and the generosity of the community, as well as some of their current needs and prayers. He seemed most concerned about his own health, for as beautiful a region as his city was, it was too warm for his poor lungs, and he often had considered moving north where the climate was more conducive to asthmatic breathing.

"I would be glad to speak to Brother Fernando on your behalf," Sister Diana compassionately offered, referencing a devoted man who was originally from Spain but often traveled to many parts to recruit young men to become priests and bishops.

"Ah, Brother Fernando," Father Antonio said, his face wreathed with smiles. "Yes, I have already spoken to him and keep up a regular correspondence with him. He has proposed a fine young man to take my place who is just finishing up his teaching but—" here he hesitated and shook his head, tears coming to his eyes, "—it all comes down to the fact that I love my people and do not wish to go. I would rather die here, among them, than go north and live in comfort but be separated from my dear people."

At that, Sister Diana pressed his hand and encouraged him to trust in the Lord, for if that was the wish of his heart, then the Lord would give him strength to continue in that manner. "Perhaps, this new brother may come and assist you, and you will not need to leave."

"Yes, yes," Father Antonio said, wiping away his tears. "Perhaps that is the best. I must be humble, too. I must not be a greedy old man and keep all of the ministry to myself."

Some time later, after showing them about the parish and about to bid farewell to the two sisters, Father Antonio looked straight at Regina, who had remained quiet and attentive the whole while. He smiled at her, then looked at Sister Diana knowingly, and then gazed back at Regina.

"God bless you, Sister Diana," he said quietly, taking the older nun's hand. "You have been a great comfort to me. Please come join us in fellowship on the day after tomorrow for our afternoon meal."

"God bless you, Father," Sister Diana returned, "and may His peace be upon you."

"God bless you, Sister Gina," Father Antonio said, turning to Regina and taking her hand as well, "and may you find all the hopes and dreams of your heart here in our little city."

"What did he mean by that?" Regina wondered aloud to Sister Diana on their way back to the camp. "It seemed like such an odd thing for a Father to say."

"I wondered that myself," Sister Diana admitted, "but the ways of God are mysterious and not beyond our human hopes and dreams." She turned and looked directly at Regina. "What do you hope for, above all else?"

At being asked that so directly, Regina blushed and looked down, not knowing what to say.

"Do not be ashamed," Sister Diana said calmly. "Search your heart and acknowledge your deepest hopes and dreams before our gracious Lord, who is willing and able to purify them and bring them to pass. Is it to say your vows and become a sister? Is it to go back home and be with your family? Or perhaps it is for marriage and children? Or perhaps it is something entirely different?"

Regina thought for a moment, her mind traveling back to her uncle Geraldo and Tomaso, the villa with the Bertolli family and Luigi, and then settling on Catarina and her two little children. "I do not know," she confessed. "There is something there, but I do not know what it is."

Sister Diana smiled a bit and took her hand, and they walked on together.

"I want to do everything, but nothing very glamorous at the same time," Regina heard herself admitting. "But I do not know what that looks like. I think that this life is very good, perhaps not the best, but what else does the Lord want me to do?"

Sister Diana did not reply until just before they reached the camp. Then she turned and smiled kindly at Regina. "Remain before the Lord with your deepest heart's desires. Be honest with Him and submit to His leading. He will show you the best way, whatever it may be."

Part Six

Several days later, Sister Diana, Sister Anna, and Regina returned to Father Antonio's church where they had been invited to partake in the afternoon meal. The whole group had been invited, but the other sisters were eager to return to the contacts they had made earlier in the week.

"I met this lovely young woman," Sister Anna was saying as they approached the church, "who I very much believe that you, Sister Gina, would greatly enjoy conversing with. I will introduce you to her, and perhaps you may be of some encouragement to her."

"I, also, wish to talk with her," Sister Diana said, upon hearing about the particular struggle that the woman was facing after being in a marriage that her family did not approve of.

Upon arriving at the church, Sister Anna excused herself to speak with Father Antonio after pointing out the young woman in question. At that, Sister Diana took Regina by the hand and led her over to a table where a young woman with blonde hair was talking to a dark-haired man. Regina's heart immediately leaped in her chest, but she restrained herself as Sister Diana pulled out a chair for herself and motioned for Regina to sit down as well.

The young woman introduced herself as Georgina de Lucca and then held out a soft, delicate hand toward her companion. "This is my husband's good friend, Brother Luigi."

The man politely greeted Sister Diana, but when he looked straight at Regina, it seemed that his gaze held her for an eternity. Sister Diana immediately began talking to Georgina and Brother Luigi rose to sit closer to Regina, introducing himself as if they had never met before.

Regina also remained calm and acted as if she had never seen this man before, but even to the casual observer, it remained evident that the dark eyes of the handsome Luigi never left Regina's face for a moment, and that the pink blush upon her cheeks and her demure attitude remained as long as he gave her his attentions.

After dinner and meeting many other kind and generous people, Regina found Sister Diana still talking to Georgina and quietly excused herself, saying that she needed to return to the camp and help Catarina care for the children that evening. Sister Diana looked at Regina carefully and then smiled, nodding her permission.

Regina saw Luigi across the room, talking to several men. She dared not approach him to say farewell. In fact, she was glad for the opportunity to slip out unawares so that she would not need to endure the pain of separation again.

That evening, just as Regina finished bathing the children by the riverbank, she heard a rustling in the bushes behind her. Turning, she spotted Luigi standing by the line of trees, looking about to see if it was safe to come and speak with her. Catarina had just begun to herd her two little ones back toward camp, leaving Regina momentarily alone.

Regina's clothes were damp from the splashing and fun that the children enjoyed while washing, so she turned from Luigi in embarrassment, untying the skirts from her knees and crouching down to pick up her shawl to wrap once more around her neck and shoulders.

Luigi approached her, undeterred. He reached out and turned her around to face him. "Why are you afraid of me, Gina?"

"It's too dangerous for you to be here," she whispered, trembling at his touch. She drew back to look at his tanned face, his dark curly hair, and the way he smiled at her. Then she tied the shawl securely about her shoulders as if to protect herself from him.

He faced her silently and then reached out again, taking her hands in his and beginning to talk. He told her about his family, how his brother had left and returned with a new woman. He mentioned how Filippo begged their Papa to give him the villa and force Luigi to leave, which had only resulted in Papa becoming angry and leaving with Mama and Grandmamma to go live with the cousins, putting a curse upon the whole household.

Luigi also told her how he had tried to bring peace to his family but finally gave up and left to work with Brother Andre. Then, after a long and busy winter, he resolved to find her and spent the long spring months on that quest.

"I cannot tell you how I have suffered every night, Gina," he told her, "thinking of how I may have made a mistake in sending you away, how you might have been hurt, how you may very well be alone and friendless in the world. I am overjoyed and thankful to our gracious Father to see you alive and well."

She smiled at him a bit timidly, surprised to see how much he still cared for her. She felt unsure what this meant for her ministry with the sisters. "But what about your work with Brother Andre?" she wondered.

Luigi hesitated and then admitted in a quiet and sad tone, crossing himself, "Brother Andre died over the winter, may God give rest to his soul."

"Oh!" Regina gave a short cry to hear that sad news. "But what about your family?" she pressed, hardly daring to hope that there was any possibility left for her to be with him.

"What family?" he said, his expression showing his grief. "My family, or what is left, lies in tatters back in San Paolo. Gina, you are all I have left as a friend in the world."

"And no one else?" Regina wondered, her lower lip trembling slightly.

"There are some others, of course," Luigi said dismissively. "The Lord never leaves His children friendless, and I know many caring brothers and sisters—but none like you," he quickly added. He gazed into her timid eyes for a moment and then asked, "Would you not have me as a friend?"

"I would," Regina said, still trembling in her passion, "and I would have you as a friend to me as well, but how can this ever be possible? I am living as a sister, even though my uncle will not permit me to take holy vows, and his hired hand is constantly watching me. He said he would contact me in the spring, but he has not, and I fear the evil plans he may have prepared for me."

Luigi was quiet for a moment as he left her side and walked up and down the riverbank, looking in all directions at their surroundings. Finally, he turned back to find Regina standing still and alone, tears trickling down her cheeks.

"Do not cry, Gina," he said gently, embracing her. "Go back to your camp and eat your supper and help with the evening work and pretend that you will go to sleep with the rest of them. But pack your things and meet me here at midnight."

"What will you do?" Regina asked, drying her eyes with her shawl.

"My good friend Brother Gregorio and his wife left for Australia two years ago because of the great needs in that region. He has begged and begged me for over a year to come and help with the work there. We will go together, if you will come, and we will work there freely as husband and wife."

"Australia?" she said in surprise, gazing at him. "That is so far away."

"It will be a long journey, but we will be together, and we will be free." He gazed at her for a long moment and then asked quietly, "Will you come?"

She hesitated for just a moment and then nodded, releasing his hand. "I will come at midnight," she said softly and turned to go.

Luigi followed her and caught her at the woods line. "Gina!" he said passionately.

Regina turned back to him, a question in her eyes.

He reached out and kissed her. "I will wait for you," he said quietly, bidding her to go quickly. "God be with you and grant you safety and peace."

She left him at that and headed back to her camp. As Regina walked, she gazed all around her at the dimming world of yellow, green, and blue, wondering how it was that she would never see this part of the world again. As excited as she was to leave, it was strange to suddenly realize that the uncertainty of this chapter of her life was coming to a swift end.

Part Seven

Regina sat around the fire and watched all the sisters and the little children eat their suppers. She thought about how she would miss them all and how they would also miss her. She had the fleeting thought of whether what she was doing in making such a decision in going with Luigi to Australia was wrong in God's eyes. She sat there at the fire, quietly staring into the flame, long after Sister Anna gave the evening blessing and they all began retiring to their tents for the night.

Regina rose at last, going to Sister Diana's tent, kneeling down to look and see if the woman was there. Sister Diana was lying down, but Sister Anna was still kneeling in prayer and saw Regina.

Motioning for her to come in, Sister Anna said kindly, "What is it, Sister Gina? You have been quiet all evening. What troubles you?"

Regina felt a bit awkward, never feeling quite comfortable around Sister Anna for how direct she was, preferring the gentler ways of Sister Diana. She hesitated for a bit, her head bowed, and then looked up to see Sister Anna back at her prayers and Sister Diana sitting up, patiently waiting for an answer.

"Father Antonio said that God may bring my hopes and dreams to me here in Speranza," Regina began timidly, "and you," here she looked at Sister Diana, "told me to bring my secret thoughts to God for Him to purify and bring to pass."

Sister Anna broke off her prayers and looked pointedly at Regina. "Brother Luigi Bertolli?" she asked directly.

"Anna," Sister Diana said in a gentle rebuke, seeing how Regina's face flushed as she dropped her head. "Sister Gina," she went on quietly, "Brother Luigi has told us all that he knows about you, and we have spoken to Father Antonio. If our gracious Lord is calling you to serve Him in Australia, and that is your heart's desire to be with Brother Luigi, then go in peace."

"You knew?" Regina said in amazement. "You know everything?"

Sister Diana smiled slightly, shaking her head at Sister Anna as the latter suddenly cackled in glee. Then Diana gently explained, "Sister Antoinette has been in contact with Brother Luigi since the first time he arranged for you to escape an unwanted marriage and join us. That is how he knew where to find you here, in the city of Speranza."

"Oh." Regina sat still, a bit dumbfounded. "So, everything was arranged without me knowing about it?"

"The Lord arranged all of the details," Sister Diana corrected. "We were only His willing servants."

"Of course, we did not know that you would agree so readily," Sister Anna added, her tone sharp as she shook her head at Regina disapprovingly. "I thought at least you would need convincing that this was the right thing to do. Were I in your shoes, I would not have agreed so readily. Are you leaving with him tonight?"

"Anna," Sister Diana rebuked her again. Smiling at Regina, she leaned forward and took her hand. "Go in peace, Sister Gina, we are assured of God's graces upon you. Brother Luigi is a good man and will keep you safe."

At that, Regina felt a flood of emotion and rushed forward into Sister Diana's arms. "I will miss you," she said with sudden tears. "I do not know what life will be like without you."

Sister Diana held the young woman tightly in her arms and then kissed her on the forehead. "Our gracious heavenly Father will provide another family for you. The community under Brother Gregorio is a very dear one indeed, and you will be at home there. Go in peace, my sister."

Regina drew back to leave at that, but suddenly, Sister Anna was plucking her sleeve and handing her a soft cloth package.

"What is this?" Regina wondered, unfolding the cloth to find a small wooden cross with a worn leather strap. She looked at Sister Anna in surprise. "Where did you find this? I thought I had lost it at Santa Maria!"

"You did lose it, providentially speaking," Sister Anna said with a twinkle in her eye. "I took it, since we needed some way to prove to Brother Luigi that you were the same Regina he was searching for. Sister Maria said it was your most prized possession, and now we know why."

"Anna," Sister Diana said wearily. "Let the poor child go, and do not torment her any longer."

Sister Anna smiled at that. "Go in peace, Sister Gina, and may God's grace go with you."

Regina returned to her own tent, finding Catarina and the children already asleep. Of all the dear people she loved in the group, she felt saddest to leave them behind. Yet, she was assured that the mother and her young ones would be fine with each other, the sisters, and the many townsfolk who would all support and care for them.

She lay down quietly, holding the wooden cross on her chest and thinking for a long time about everything that had transpired over the past months of her life. Regina listened to the sounds of the camp going to sleep for the night, praying silently that the journey ahead would go well. All she needed to do was patiently wait for the last three hours to pass before it was time for her to rejoin Luigi and remain with him forever.

CHAPTER FIVE

The Rascal

His name was Jedidiah Coopers, but he insisted on being called plain Jed. Every day of his life, he had faced his mother telling him, "God loves you, Jedidiah. Beloved by the Lord Almighty, that's what your name means, son of my body."

"My name is Jed!" he always raged in reply.

Early one month, in the peculiar season between fall and winter when the farm fields lay sullen and quiet, Jed turned eighteen. He woke that morning with the realization that he was now his own man, and no one could tell him any longer that his responsibility lay solely with the family and the farm.

That morning, he came downstairs with his belongings determinedly tossed over his shoulder and marched from the house without so much as a goodbye to anyone except the dog. His siblings gaped on from the frost-bitten windows, and his father sat at the table as the big door slammed shut over the windy cold. His mother was praying in her bedroom and got up from her knees, wailing, and ran after him, but Jed walked on, whistling. Just like that.

"I don't have anything to look back on," he told the stranger in the old horse-drawn wagon who picked him up two miles down the road, far from his sobbing mother. "All she did was nag, nag, nag, and then preach when nothing else worked. I'm a man now. I got to make my own living."

The weathered old man chewed on the piece of straw sticking out from between his lips, his hat bobbing as the old horse plodded on. He said nothing, but there was a sparkle in his eye that showed something, perhaps amusement at Jed's youth, perhaps wisdom from his old age.

Jed rambled on and on as the wagon took them both toward civilization. "I already got my eye on a shop. You know that smithy in the middle of town? He offered me a job once, and I'll take it. I'm kind of old for starting an apprenticeship, but I'm strong, and I can do the work.

I've been working on the farm too long. It's time for my brothers to take over."

The old man lifted his eyebrows but still said nothing.

"Yeah, my dad's there, too, but he doesn't care. My mother, she'll yell at me something fierce after she gets her crying out, and she'll preach to me and try to make me go back, but not my dad. He'll just come out and visit, and then he'll let me be, you'll see."

They had reached the edge of the town, and Jed was in a hurry to get moving. The old nag was too slow for him.

"I'll be along now," he said to the silent figure beside him. "Thanks for the ride, Gramps."

The old man turned from staring down the road and prodded the young man's arm with a gnarled finger.

Jed looked up in surprise.

"You be smart now, youngster," he said with a wise wink of a rheumy eye. "The world ain't as welcoming as you think. Best not to forget those who really love you."

"I know, I know," Jed said with a bit of impatience. He sprang off the wagon and then tipped his cap to the old man. "Thanks for the ride!" he yelled over the noise of the blowing cold and then walked off jauntily. What did an old man know about life and being loved? Jed was his own man now, after all.

J ed had many friends in town, and he felt quite at home away from his family. There was the green grocer, the new cobbler who recently set up shop, the smithy, the lady at the school, and the kind folks at the church. His family always attended the church in the other town, since it was more holy, according to his mother. Jed preferred this church instead for its high steeple and the tall priest clothed in flowing garbs, followed by boys and their candles, incense, and prayers. He stared at the church as he went past, his feet pointed toward the smithy.

"Hello, Jed."

He glanced up casually and then froze in surprise. It was Father John's niece, the sweet little Caroline who used to sit next to him in Bible class. He was forever jumping up in his chair and blurting out the wrong answers while she primly sat beside him, raising her eyebrows in surprise and writing down the correct answers in her notebook. He thought she was too well-behaved for her own good, but she was related to the priest after all, so she had that obligation.

But now, here she was in front of him, all grown up. Her hair was neatly tied up under a thick scarf and her rosy lips and cheeks smiled at him in the cold, but her eyes were as wise and innocent as they always had been. As he continued to gape at her, she looked at him with a bit of puzzlement and perhaps even bemusement but said nothing further.

"Well, hi, Carrie," Jed said at last in an important tone of voice, sticking his thumbs in his pockets and puffing out his chest like he was a dignitary. The bag containing his worldly possessions began to swing back and forth absently from its perch on his shoulder.

"Where are you off to?" she asked mildly, an empty basket resting on her arm.

"Oh, see the world, get a job, make a living, that sort of thing," he replied, still on his high horse.

She nodded and glanced past him. "How is your family?"

"Fine." He gazed down the street. As pretty as she was, Jed was eager to get on. He had no time for those who looked back in the past on their ancestry and were forever attached to home.

"Good. Well, have a nice day, Jed. I must be back at the parsonage. We have some more baked goods to deliver."

Jed merely nodded and stepped off the sidewalk momentarily to let her pass. A do-gooder, that Caroline Sentry, just like her mother and her father. But he remembered her uncle the priest and the fun conversations they always had about war and worldwide scandals.

"Say hello to your uncle Father John for me!" he shouted over his shoulder, far too loudly for the short distance between them.

She glanced back, raised her eyebrows just like she did in class, and merely nodded. "I am certain that he extends his greetings to you, also, and your family. Good day, Jed."

Jed sniffed impatiently and moved on down the road. Forever talking about family, these people. It was time for all of them to grow up, he thought. Shaking such things from his mind, he greeted a couple of men walking across the road from the mill, a stout piece of lumber across their shoulders.

"Need some help?" he immediately asked.

The lead man sized up the boy quickly and then said a bit gruffly, "No, lad, just hurry on out of the way."

Stepping aside, Jed shrugged and moved on down to the smithy. He beamed as he approached, thinking of old man Hendrickson and his stout wife who always had many lovely things baking in her oven. Not to forget, of course, their charming, giggly daughter and their spritely school lad who was always a lot of fun when he was home.

As expected, the family welcomed Jed heartily and immediately took up his offer to work for them. Not that they particularly needed the help, but Ralph Hendrickson was growing older and appreciated a young man to run errands for him when his own lad was not around.

Of course, blacksmithing was also a good trade to learn and would prove profitable once Jed became experienced in the craft. At least that was what the old man said. His wife naturally agreed, as she served him up fresh squash bread and cool milk from the dairy. All the while, their tall and shapely daughter tittered and batted her eyelashes at the young man from across the room.

Jed sat down at the table and leaned back in his chair comfortably. Yes, this is where he would make his home, and a good place it would be.

As the months steadily marched on and the first signs of spring began to show, Jed decided that he would make the little village his permanent home.

Meanwhile, old man Hendrickson boasted of his new apprentice throughout the town, saying that Jed was a fast learner, a natural at the blacksmithing trade, and would certainly take over the little shop one day. The church also accepted Jed as one of their own as he became a faithful attendee, worshipping right alongside the best and worst of them and finding great solace and comfort in doing so.

Jed rightly suspected his family would come visit now and again, but he was relieved that his mother was always quiet and subdued in the presence of the town folk. After putting in an order of lumber for a new barn, his father once stopped to watch Jed hammer out horseshoes for the big work horses, but he didn't say much except to inquire how business was going. Jed appreciated that because it made him feel like a man.

As if town membership and good business were not enough to make him a man, Jed's progress with the womenfolk was also quite encouraging. He decided after a week or two at the Hendricksons' that their daughter Ruby was quite a catch, but sometimes he found their courtship to be a bit slow for his fast-paced plans. So, he began visiting the schoolhouse after his daily work was done in an effort to spend some time with the schoolmarm, Miss Tina. Though she already had a beau, that fellow was traveling out west for several months, and she did not mind the additional attention. As if those two were not enough, Jed also enjoyed the companionship of various other town females, from the young girls fresh out of school to the women passing by on the streets.

Of course, there was one female Jed did not appreciate, which was that Caroline Sentry from church. Although he attended every Sunday meeting, especially all throughout the Lenten season, he tried avoiding her at all costs. Frequently, she greeted him and the Hendrickson family as she stood in the foyer with her younger siblings, waiting for the rest of her family to finish talking with the parishioners so they could walk home and she could serve them lunch. He merely nodded to her and passed on with the stately Ruby on his arm.

Little Miss Carrie was a thorn in his side, of that he was certain. One day, he passed her on the way to the schoolhouse to see Miss Tina, and she smiled at him and asked how his day was going.

"Fine," he said curtly, tipping his hat as a mere courtesy. He did not bother to ask her how *she* was doing, so she did not say.

Instead, she asked, looking at him keenly, "Do I bother you that much, Jed? You always look so displeased when-ever—"

"Oh, shut up," he said rudely, interrupting her. "Just because we were kids in Sunday school together doesn't mean we should be friends now. I have plenty of friends."

Her expressive eyebrows shot up as she quietly replied, "All right." He was relieved to have gotten off so easily, even with all his stinging words, but he wondered if she was the type to go and cry to her mama. No, he did not expect that she was, but he carefully avoided her father for the next several weeks out of precaution.

On Palm Sunday, in the midst of the joy and shouts of praise that filled the town, Jed found himself in a personal and particularly special tumult of excitement. It involved an introduction to a town visitor, one red-haired young lady by the name of Audrey, who immediately took a liking to the strong and handsome young man. After the church luncheon, the two decided to take a short stroll through the town and become better acquainted.

"Do you know that you have the most beautiful hair I have ever seen?" Jed murmured to that precocious female as she giggled upon his arm. Becoming rather engrossed in a close study of her freckles as they walked along, it was not until she gave him a sudden shove that he looked up and realized that he had nearly led her off the path into a large puddle.

"And who are those children staring at us?" Audrey wanted to know, glancing over her shoulder at the house they had just passed.

Jed said that he was certain he did not know, but long after he left Audrey at her place, he felt suspicion and displeasure growing steadily in his mind. His raging thoughts did not give him a moment's peace until he marched straightway to the front door of the parsonage.

Caroline Sentry and her siblings were still sitting upon the porch, listening to the littlest one recite her catechism. Jed waited nearby, leaning casually against the post until the book was closed and Caroline allowed them all to leave.

Rising, she looked down at the impatient young man, her expression a bit curious but also grieved.

"What's the matter with you and your kids?" he mocked, his eyes throwing sparks. "Never saw a bit of courting before?"

"Oh, Jed," she merely said, the sad look never leaving her face.

He felt uncomfortable at that and gazed down at the ground. When he lifted his head, she had come down off the steps and was standing right in front of him, her eyes searching his face. Jed backed away, his discomfort growing.

"You know," she said slowly, "there is always grace found at the foot of the cross. You know that, don't you?" When he didn't answer, she persisted. "Don't you know that, Jed?"

"Yeah, I know it," he said and turned away roughly, marching all the way back to the Hendricksons' for dinner. He sat beside Ruby, as he always did, and laughed and smiled more than he ever did in his life. It was a beautiful spring day.

The beauty of spring continued straight through Holy Week. Every evening, Jed faithfully attended the church services, even though most of the town's folk did not bother until Good Friday.

On Thursday, he found himself in one of the front pews where all the foot-washing was taking place. Normally, he scoffed at such things, but today he was especially feeling that this was where he was supposed to be. It had been an excellent day in the smithy and, after doing a few odds and ends for the schoolmarm, he had gone home to help Ruby prepare a delicious dinner for the family. After all of his hard work, he thought he deserved some appreciation of his own. Christ the Lord certainly would wash Jed's feet along with the rest of the disciples.

Jed stared up at the great cross looming above the altar, lost in thought about the majesty of the Lord's sacrifice, when a shadow crossed his path. There was a moment of mutual surprise when Jed's eyes rested upon the face of Caroline Sentry as she came to stop in front of him.

"Jed? You are here?" she said in surprise, a brief smile lighting her face as she shifted the basin of water she carried so that it did not splash her dress.

He felt a sudden wave of embarrassment, wishing he had put on clean socks before coming to church. He imagined he was far away from church, anywhere away where he did not have to see the innocent gaze of her blue eyes. But his pants seemed glued to the seat, preventing him from getting up and moving or even saying anything as the horror of his imagination continued to roll over him.

Not her. She would never wash his feet. She would see the scars. The scars from when his father had thrown a boiling kettle of water to the floor in anger. The scars from when his mother had whipped the backs of his legs and ankles for saying something inappropriate to a little girl cousin. The scars from his going over the scabs and picking at them in bitterness. She would see them, and she would wonder why the scars were there. She would ask why he hadn't done anything about them or gone to the doctor. He clenched his fists tighter as he heard her say something else, and he wished that he could be gone and far away from her, never, ever to return.

"Surely He hath borne our griefs and carried our sorrows, yet we did esteem Him stricken, smitten of God, and afflicted."

It was his mother's voice. Jed glanced around, but she was not there.

"But He was wounded for our transgressions, He was bruised for our iniquities, the chastisement of our peace was upon Him, and with His stripes we are healed."

Jed shook his head and looked up at Caroline, but she was silent, allowing him to decide the way that he would take.

"All we like sheep have gone astray, we have turned every one to his own way, and the Lord hath laid on Him the iniquity of us all."

If only the words would stop! He did not come here to hear preaching!

"Jed?"

He looked up at Caroline, seeing her as if for the first time.

She smiled slightly, reassuringly. "There is always mercy and grace found at the foot of the cross, Jed. He has taken your iniquities. You can give all your stripes to Him."

Suddenly, all of his fear and discomfort was replaced by a sense of growing rage. When he looked away from her in disdain, he heard a quiet sigh ripple all through her.

"Please, Jed," he heard as he stood suddenly, colliding with the basin she held in front of her, sending a sheet of water flying up in the air and neatly landing upon her aproned front.

He glared at her, feeling a perverse bit of relief come over him to see her dress drenched, but her expression was merely one of astonishment. Then, unexpectedly, she laughed.

At that, all Jed felt was white-hot anger, and he lashed out against her with a sudden rage. How it came to be that her head struck the step leading to the altar, he was not certain, but there she lay, directly beneath the foot of the cross. Somehow, he instinctively knew that she could not rise of her own accord.

A great murmur began somewhere to his left, and Jed felt the anger replaced by panic. Turning quickly, he hurried out of the church and ran all the way to the Hendrickson house. When he saw the light burning in the window for him to show him the way, he remembered.

"We have turned, every one to his own way."

Feeling greater panic, Jed hurried away, past the darkened shops lining the street, until he reached the schoolhouse on the edge of town. He was about to rap on Miss Tina's door when he remembered her beau was back in town and they were visiting friends for the evening. There was no place to go except the plains, and so he fled into the darkness.

Good Friday rose early and somber. The whole town carried a dark pall, from the great tragedy that had befallen the beloved Caroline to the sudden disappearance of the young man Jed. That evening, there was much weeping in the church, save for one corner in which the runaway stood, stone-faced and angry. He did not understand God, much less His Son who came and died for the sinner. Jed did not want to be saved.

He left in the middle of the service, fuming, and went to the parsonage, banging on the door. Little Jenny came, white-faced, to the door.

"Where's Carrie?" he demanded, staring down at her.

"In bed," the little one lisped.

He pushed his way into the house and looked around, as if he would go and see her.

Jenny gasped. "You can't! Mama said to call her if anything happened and not to let in any visitors!"

Jed stopped, deciding to take it slow with the child. "What happened?" he asked, bending down and gently taking the girl's hands in his.

Jenny's eyes widened, but she calmed down. "Some mean person hurt her," she said, frowning in condemnation. "Someone hurt her, and she fell down and broke her neck, so she can't walk. She has to go to a doctor far, far away." Tears formed in her eyes and the sweet face crumpled. "I want Carrie to get better," the girl suddenly wept, throwing herself into Jed's arms.

"There, there," he said awkwardly. "It will be all right." He patted her back and then eased her away from him. "Can I go see her? I'll be quiet."

The little one hesitated.

"Jenny?" a weak voice called from the back bedroom. "Who is there?"

"It's Jed!" Jenny replied in a clear, high voice. "Do you want to talk to him?"

After a great quiet came a soft, "Yes."

Jed got up slowly and patted Jenny's soft curly head before walking carefully into the bedroom, his hat in his hand. He stopped in the doorway, shocked to see how pale and listless Caroline looked. Her head and neck were in a brace, but she lifted a small hand and held it out to him.

He went to her, trembling, afraid that she would say something that he deserved to hear. But he took her hand and sat down carefully in the chair by her bed.

"Jed," she said quietly, in a whisper.

He hung his head, waiting, her cool fingers grasping his.

"I forgive you."

He looked up, startled, and withdrew his hand from hers. Not again. How was it that she always did that which was most unexpected? He searched her face but only saw the clear, blue-eyed innocence and the wisdom that went far beyond her years.

In his mind's eye, he could suddenly see himself kneeling at her bed, weeping and sobbing. He could hear his repentant words coming out in a rush, unintelligible and honest. But he simply sat there for a long time, silent and unable to move because of the grief brought by the knowledge of his great transgressions.

He came to himself when he felt a little hand slip into his. He opened his eyes and saw Jenny standing next to him, tears rolling down her little cheeks. Lifting his head,

Jed looked at Caroline, and her eyes met his quickly, as if she had been waiting.

"There is *always* grace and forgiveness found at the foot of the cross, Jed," she said, firmly and decisively.

"Are you sure?" he asked.

"Yes, I am sure." Then a sad look came to her face, and her eyes drifted away from his face.

He rose to his feet and bent over her. "Carrie?"

She seemed faraway, her gaze transfixed on something distant. "Jedidiah Cooper," she was saying quietly, reflectively. "Jed, you need to realize something."

"What?" he asked, resisting the urge to shake her to full alertness, knowing it would hurt her. "Carrie, what? Wake up!"

Her eyes returned to his and she smiled. "Jed, you need to remember. God loves you very much. He has made you, He has saved you, He has loved you."

"Oh." He felt a bit troubled by the simplicity of that statement, but at the same time, he felt a bit relieved. If she said it, it must be true. She always had the right answers in Bible class. He looked back at her. "Carrie?"

"But you must believe."

"I don't know," he suddenly stammered. "I don't know how to, but I do—I do want to believe."

"Do you?" Joy suddenly shone in her eyes. "Good. Then, talk to Father—and Uncle John. They will teach you the Bible, the promises of God."

Jed was not sure. "Are they angry with me?"

"Angry?" Her voice was so faint. Then she laughed and a bit of strength came back to her. "Oh, Jed, you have always been loved by many people. By God—"

"I know that," he interrupted impatiently. "But is your family angry?"

"You have always been loved by your family, too," she said, as if she did not hear him. "They are not angry."

Jed felt a bit of irritation at her mention of his family. What was it that his mother always said about him as the son of her body and the Lord God Almighty? Whatever it was, he did not need to know, and he certainly did not want to think about his family.

"My family—" her voice was fading again and her eyes were closing, as if she was going to sleep.

"Yes?" he leaned closer to her, concerned, not wanting to miss a word. "Carrie?" he called to her. "What about your family?"

Her eyes drifted open. "You have been loved by my family, too." Her gaze held him a second, and then she smiled and closed her eyes. "And by—well, by me, also."

Jed stood up away from her in shock. "You?"

"Yes, Jed," she said, her voice fading as she drifted away in sleep. "You have always been loved by everyone, now you simply need to be loved, Jed—"

His eyes suddenly filled with tears, sending him stumbling to the door, blinded, nearly falling down the steps as he left, ignoring little Jenny who called out to him.

What was it that his mother always recited? Caroline had said, "Be loved, Jed." Yes, that was it. That was what his mother had always said. She had always said that his name meant beloved. Beloved by the Lord God Almighty.

Jed could stand the pressure no longer. Bursting into a sob, he charged toward the darkness of the cool night and began running down the road. He wept louder as he ran faster, as if hounds were on his trail and would soon catch up to him.

Some of the town's folk heard the noise and peered out into the darkness, surprised to see a boy hardly a man running for all he was worth toward the farmlands and screaming with all his might, "Mama!"

CHAPTER SIX

The Unexpected Threat

Lucy was a bit of a conundrum. When inquired upon, she hesitantly acknowledged that she was pretty as far as appearances went, but to the rest of the seeing world, she was unquestionably beautiful. Naturally, not every single person in her circles viewed her as such, for women in particular are apt to criticize beauty with a more judgmental eye, but for the most part, Lucy was known to be physically flawless. Furthermore, her timidity only served to make her beauty even more rare and charming.

As a rule, Lucy was a gentlewoman in the true sense of the word. Unlike most married ladies, she never quite grew out of her child-like sweetness or girlish bashfulness. On the first morning of the month of August, her twentieth birthday and wedding coincided, and the villagers all agreed that she made the most perfect and most glorious bride ever to have stood before their church's golden altar. Now, quite some years later, her appearance had not changed a bit. She was still viewed in much of the same vein, as perfect and untouchable as a porcelain doll.

On this particular day, Lucy sat at her familiar spot, behind a sewing machine in the seamstress's shop. While still the most beautiful, she was quickly becoming all the more timid and reclusive. Her first and only love was working down the street at the lumber mill, having suddenly arrived four autumns ago from the Wild West to sweep her off her feet the following spring and marry her that very summer. Now, they lived in a frugal little apartment in the village, their lives appearing to work together quite nicely like a hand fitting into a well-shaped glove, but not all was perfect.

For all her beauty and marital happiness, Lucy suffered from an acute sort of loneliness and sadness that could not easily be explained. As time had slowly gone by after the wedding and the excitement of first love had died down, the world looked and felt different. Perhaps everyone, including her jovial husband, saw her as exactly the same woman as before, but she often told herself in the most private of moments that she felt like a nervous bird, wings all atremble as if she would suddenly fly off the tenuous branch she had just landed upon.

So Lucy lived, and had lived for the past two years, in a state of invisible apprehension and loneliness while still maintaining an outward appearance of happiness and loveliness. She kept her thoughts to herself, hidden and deep where they could be undisturbed in their loneliness.

Today, however, was an ordinary Tuesday in early winter, and Lucy thought of none of these things as she sat upon the stool before the sewing machine. Her quick little fingers guided the material around the hopping needle and she worked steadily, not bothering to look out at the flakes softly drifting down from the pregnant sky or the snow-covered hats of the villagers trotting by the shop window.

Lucy stopped at the end of the sleeve to snip off a navy line and rise, lifting the garment from the desk and giving it one quick shake, allowing the loose thread-ends and fabric crumbs to fall to the wide-board floor below. It was a man's shirt, blue plaid and cozy warm for the cold winter months.

Her employer, Mistress Margaret McCauley, was busy racketing away at her own clicking machine in between loudly settling accounts with the patrons that swept in and out of the door on an hourly basis.

Hearing the mistress noisily complaining to a customer about the oncoming snowstorm, Lucy's eyes curiously drifted to the window. Without even noticing the steady fall of crystal flakes, she was shocked to find a pair of strangers steadily watching her.

One fellow was short and slender, dressed smartly from his boot tops to his chin with a neat wool cap atop his golden curls. A gloved hand gently stroked the carefully trimmed beard upon his cheeks and chin as he spoke to his companion.

The other man was much taller and a bit stouter, his face red from the cold but appearing to take no great precautions to protect his bodily person from the elements as the other had done. His only protection from the cold wind was a great overcoat that was not even buttoned up and a top hat that was rakishly ajar on top of his head.

Lucy looked from one to the other and then immediately felt shy. She curtseyed a bit, out of mere politeness, and then put her back to the window as she set the plaid shirt back down on the sewing machine table and began to arrange it for hemming.

Not two minutes later, the approaching sound of boots upon the wood floor caused Lucy to glance up. She immediately recognized the two fellows who had just been standing outside her window. Her hands lowered from the shirt to her lap, and she held them together so that they did not visibly tremble.

"Good afternoon, ma'am," the shorter fellow greeted politely, doffing his cap but making no inquiries and not showing any sign of departure from his post in front of her desk. His companion had already completed his survey of Lucy, the shirt, and the machine, and he was now quickly scanning the bolts of materials against the wall and making his way toward the shelves of shirts and other garments that had not yet been sold.

"Hello, sir," Lucy replied shyly, rising quickly and standing there under the first fellow's blue-eyed gaze. She noticed that they were both gentlemen of wealth, based upon the quality and particular material of their coats, which caused her to hesitate a moment before sitting down to resume her work.

The two men then came together in the middle of the room, talking to one another in low voices and nodding pleasantly as they glanced again in her direction.

"May I help you find anything, sirs?" Lucy asked when they paused from their talk and returned to her side.

"No, ma'am," the shorter man replied with a golden smile as he bowed slightly in a more formal greeting. "Alfred Brisson, ma'am, and we are visiting Camden, which seems to be a fascinating little village, I dare say. Reminds me of home, up north. My companion—"

"Thomas Walton," the second fellow said in his deep voice with a similar bow, but he offered no further explanation.

Lucy smiled slightly, curtseying again and politely replying, "Welcome to Camden, sirs."

"Thank you, ma'am." Brisson bowed slightly again. "And may I ask whom we have the pleasure of addressing?"

She faltered for a second and then said shyly, "Lucy—Mrs. Lucy Dalton. I am but a seamstress here." Her gaze returned to the shirt she was finishing as she thought of how displeased Mistress Margaret McCauley would be to find her distracted from her work. Lucy hoped that the men would take the hint of her great responsibilities at hand and depart at last.

"Please, ma'am, do not mind us," Brisson quickly said, smiling once again. "We shall not interrupt your excellent work. It was merely that, well, in passing by, we chanced to see you through the window and found your skill and handling of the sewing machine rather," he paused momentarily, glancing at his companion, "well, rather extraordinary."

Lucy unintentionally blushed and sat down. While she was somewhat used to hearing about her rare beauty, it had been quite some time since the world made mention of her skills, and that especially from men of the world who were well-dressed and much wealthier than she ever hoped to be. Her bashfulness preventing her from answering, Lucy merely bent her brow to the desk and busied herself in the final task of smoothing and snipping.

She rose some moments later, the garment in hand completed, save for the buttons that Mistress Margaret McCauley would sew on herself, being extremely particular about such details. Lucy warily noticed that Brisson and Walton were still in the shop, though they had removed themselves from her immediate vicinity and seemed to be deep in conversation once again. She eyed them thoughtfully and even gently, feeling a certain curiosity toward them for showing her, she supposed, undue kindness.

As if feeling her timid glance, the men turned as one from the display rack. Brisson bestowed upon her another golden smile for which he was soon becoming famous.

Then Walton said without hesitation, "What an excellent shirt. Pray tell me, ma'am, how much do you charge for such a garment?"

"Why," Lucy said in bewilderment, "it is not even finished, sir. The buttons still need sewn on, and it needs pressed, and—"

"Please, ma'am," Brisson interrupted her gently with a slight motion of a gloved hand. "Do not trouble yourself. If we wish to make a purchase, another shirt will be just as fine." He smiled at his companion and then faced her again to ask, "Tell me, ma'am, how long have you been employed at this fine establishment?"

"Well," Lucy replied uncertainly, the blush rising in her cheeks once more, finding their kindly attentiveness quite unnerving. "Well, about two and a half years now. My husband works for Gunther's Mills, and I help in this shop on a part-time basis. Some people think that it is not right for a woman to work, but Johnny and I—I mean, my husband allows me to work because I do not like being idle," she ended in confusion.

"Quite so, ma'am, and you need not trouble yourself on that account," Brisson began, but his fellow cut him off.

"Mrs. Dalton," Thomas Walton said directly, motioning to himself, "I am part of the managerial staff at Singer Manufacturing Company in New York City. My fellow and I are on a campaign to assist in the marketing of the Singer sewing machines, and we firmly believe that you would be the most able-bodied woman to assist us in our task."

"Indeed," Alfred Brisson said warmly, stepping up and handing her his business card. "Mrs. Dalton, your beauty and grace in handling the Singer sewing machine with expert deftness and agility has convinced both of us that you are exactly the person that we have been attempting to find—and for quite some time!"

Lucy took the business card with some amount of perplexity, her cheeks bright pink from their compliments. The very thought of being featured in Singer's marketing campaign caused her great surprise, but it was more than that. There was something about Mr. Brisson's blue eyes that caused her an unexpected amount of warmth.

Seeing her shyness and hesitation, Walton said to her, "Please, do discuss it with your husband, Mrs. Dalton, and consider the fortune that it will afford both of you over the years." He began to take out his own business card and appeared about to speak further.

At that moment, however, Mistress Margaret McCauley swept into the room and plucked at the elbows of both men in a commanding gesture. "My dear sirs!" she boomed in Walton's right ear with syrupy sweetness. Turning to Brisson's left ear, she continued, "Allow me to show you our finest shirt rack!"

It was not a question, quite obviously, for Mistress Margaret McCauley never asked questions. Instead, she made demands. When she was in a more genial mood, she provided suggestions. On the rare occasion, she demurred to the customer, but by and large, she made certain that every patron was aware of her position as sole proprietress of the establishment and sole judge of their wardrobe as well.

Walton appeared to glower slightly, but Brisson merely gave a helpless shrug and sent one last fleeting smile to Lucy over his shoulder as the three of them disappeared around the corner upon a sparse carpet of fabric crumbs and leftover dust from the coal stove ruffled by Mistress Margaret McCauley's billowing skirts.

Lucy gazed after the retreating figures in grave surprise, and then she sat down quickly, her hands upon her flushed cheeks in consternation. She stared at the neat little business card now resting on the sewing machine table, a thousand questions coming into her mind.

How could it be so, and for a fact, that these men would stumble upon her and believe that she, of all people, would be the perfect individual for a nationwide marketing campaign? How did she allow such men to so boldly walk into the room when they did and even allow them to take her precious time and consideration without first consulting Mistress Margaret McCauley or her husband on the matter? And, worst of all, how could it be that her natural fear and timidity that would ordinarily cause her to swiftly decline such an offer and remain a quiet seamstress in an unknown town had suddenly been driven away by the exciting temptation of fame and fortune by a most finely dressed fellow?

Indeed, the situation was most curious. Yet, what was most astounding of all was that Mistress Margaret McCauley had taken it upon herself to personally remove such persons from Lucy's immediate vicinity. Certainly, men and women wandered in and out of her sewing space quite frequently, asking her questions now and then and requesting her help at particular moments.

Ordinarily, in such cases, the headmistress paid them no mind. Was it only because these men were wealthy? Had they made known to Mistress Margaret McCauley their particular intentions? Did Mistress Margaret Mc-Cauley view them as some sort of a threat to her fine establishment? Or was it something more that her employer picked up from her demeanor?

Lucy considered these things as she slipped the little card into her side pocket and rose to set the plaid shirt aside and obtain another. She was unsure if she would talk to her Johnny about it later on, or if she would merely let the opportunity pass as a fleeting fancy.

Sitting down again to her tasks at hand, Lucy began to daydream about the possibilities despite her best intentions. As the hours passed by in busy occupation, her thoughts firmly remained fixed upon the new opportunity, leaving no room for her ordinary sadness. Even Mistress McCauley noticed a difference in Lucy's demeanor and did her very best to make certain that her employee remained focused on the necessary work of the day.

Though the situation remained tentative, the little seamstress knew by the end of the day that, if nothing else, the actions of her employer presented firm evidence that here was a genuine threat to her current state as a young and faithful wife in a quiet little village.

CHAPTER SEVEN

Hope in the Darkness

The young woman quickly went down three flights of stairs, turning her face slightly to the side when she felt the corner guard's eyes sweep over her as she passed by. Pausing in front of another security official, she lifted the identification badge and the all-important pass from where they hung around her neck. She kept her amber eyes focused on the tiled floor and only allowed her gaze to travel from his smart black boots to her small black shoes with the toes all scuffed up.

She waited until she heard the all-familiar punch on her card and then lifted her head, gently pushing her silky light brown hair out of her face as Mr. Black Boots dropped the plastic-bound badge and pass back into her waiting hand.

Stepping up to the doorway, she shifted the folders tucked underneath her right arm and watched as the tile abruptly changed to a thin brown carpet that stretched down a long hallway to her destination.

The young woman's name was Elena, or Number 551, which she had learned to accept. Sometimes, late at night, she would lie on her cot in the women's barracks and mouth particular words to herself.

"My name is Elena Margaret Johnson. I am 22 years old. I have a father and a mother, two brothers, and a great-aunt who I love dearly."

Then she would stop, stare up into the darkness, give a tired sigh, and fall asleep with some sort of jumbled-up thoughts drifting through her mind like mist blown over a field just before dawn.

Every morning, she awoke, bracing herself for the cruel blast forcing them awake into the harsh world that grinned evilly at their helpless existence. When it came, she was ready and reverted into automaton mode—dressing, eating, watching, listening, obeying. Elena was smart, so she obeyed everything they said, but she cursed herself for it.

She remembered Jackie, the restless girl who did not understand the importance of strict obedience—and then one day disappeared. To where? No one knew, but they did not ask. Instead, they continued to watch, listen, and work as they waited for some sign of hope, some possibility of redemption.

Elena now stood in front of the large gray door that led down into the storage room. She hated going down there, but her daily tasks brought her to the lower levels quite frequently. She always felt an ominous presence down in the depths of the building, even though she rarely saw any guards or other living presence on those floors.

Taking a deep breath to brace against the chill, she swiped her card and listened for the familiar click that signified the door was passable. Tugging at the metal doorknob, she peered down into the darkness, down the stairs that led to the lowest level. It was always cold down there and smelled of the brown dust that covered the concrete floor.

Glancing at the guard standing up the hallway from her, she took another deep breath and shivered as she crossed the threshold and flipped the switch that flooded the staircase with a welcome light. It was too bright at first, but it was better than the darkness, and so she went on, allowing the door to click closed behind her as she descended slowly but surely.

The dusty concrete beckoned to her as she listened warily for what she would see when she turned the corner. Eyes averted from the floor for once, Elena remembered the dark brown stains she found one morning, streaks that led from the middle of the floor to the exit door at one far corner. The support poles often had streaks as well, and sometimes the guards forgot to remove the handcuffs attached to the metal rings and their instruments of torture when they were finished using them.

All she needed to do was go quickly to the small door underneath the staircase, swipe her card, enter that dark cell, put the folders into the correct filing cabinet, and then leave just as quickly as she came. But her plan of action was suddenly arrested when she turned the corner and was confronted by the scene in front of her.

Elena appeared shocked for a moment, frozen in time like a statue, but it was only for a split second before she recovered and went on her way. But she knew living humans when she saw them, and her hands trembled as she scanned her card and passed through the doorway into the vault. Whether they were dead or alive, she did not know, but she assumed the worst since they were so still and no guards were in the vicinity.

Her chest heaved violently in her effort to control her breathing as the vault door clicked behind her. She knew exactly where the light switch was located, but she squeezed her eyelids shut and counted to ten in the pitch blackness, seeking that inner place where she could appear calm and tranquil once more.

Then, just as suddenly, Elena found her place of peace. Opening her eyelids just as she reached over and flipped the light switch, she stepped over to the correct filing cabinet and set to work organizing the stack of folders under her arm.

Her task only took a few minutes. As the last file drawer slid shut with a click under her cool fingers, Elena turned to leave the vault. The door closed behind her with a hollow sound, echoing the feeling inside of her chest as she stood stock still and took up a quick examination of the situation in front of her once again.

"Water—"

Her head jerked toward the sound, her daring eyes coming to rest upon a man with dark hair matted on his forehead, bruises on his face, one eye swollen shut, and the other orb squinting at her painfully. He half-hung, half-knelt, his hands nearly purple from the pressure of the iron shackles supporting most of his weight.

Tears blinding her eyes, Elena stumbled forward, reaching out as she passed the poles on either side of her, hoping that each person would somehow come to life while she walked to the one who had called for help. Reaching the older man, she boldly put her arms around him, lifting with an effort that seemed far beyond her natural strength. He struggled and then stood on his own.

"Water?"

"I'm sorry," she whispered, her native language dancing on the tip of her tongue, sounding like an old song that she had forgotten to sing for hundreds of years.

He shook his head and then let out a tired sigh. "It's okay."

Feeling the burning urge rise up in her chest, she wiped the tears from her cheeks. "I'll try to find something for you, okay?"

His head bobbed forward wearily, and then his forehead came to rest against the pole.

Elena stood there for a moment longer, her hand still resting on his shoulder, and then slowly turned her head to look at all of the others one by one, some of them be-yond hope, some of their eyes resting on her expectantly, hopefully, and yet wearily. There was not much hope to be seen, only a quiet kind of waiting for death to arrive that would release them from their earthly bonds.

She considered her options at that point. She was deter-mined to do something to relieve their pain, but it would require some foresight and planning. If she were caught—

Elena swallowed hard. If she attempted to help them, she would be caught. In that case, she would be punished. Perhaps she might even be killed. The details were insignif-icant, but her mind was made up.

Her eyes scanning the group once again to make a head-count, Elena's eyes suddenly widened with recognition, and she stood frozen once more. She knew him—the male figure in the back corner with the blond hair, tall and slumped over, the broad shoulders bent as if he carried the whole world on his back. Thoughts of urgency entered her mind and drove reality out of her brain.

Going forward quickly yet silently, she ignored the rest of them and their expressions of hope and desire and went to the one who caught her attention. She stood in front of him for just a moment, gazing upon him and waiting for him to notice her, but she could see that he was intently studying the floor and had the weight of the world to consider as he bravely bent his back to bear the heavy load.

"Darren?"

The man stirred from his pensive thoughts and momentarily cast off the heavy weight that rested on his strong shoulders. Weary eyes were raised to meet her searching ones, and then she was weeping silently in his arms.

The girl felt his quiet strength behind the unmeasurable exhaustion and held him close, refusing to let him go. Then she raised her head to look into his dark brown eyes, seeing the resignation behind the pain.

"It's okay," she murmured, as if trying to comfort herself instead of him. "I'll get you something to eat, and something to drink, and I'll clean off your face and all that—oh, Darren! What brutes they are!"

The man blinked and then gently shook his head, as if attempting to release himself from her hold. "Lena," he addressed her, using the nickname she had been given in childhood that he had used for her when they had been in classes together at school.

"Yes?"

"You need to leave," he said quietly.

"I know. I'll be back, I promise. I'll bring you—I'll bring all of you—"

She stopped, seeing that he was shaking his head again, the weariness and exhaustion making him appear in her eyes more like an old sage, an ancient philosopher.

"What?"

"You must go—and don't come back until you are certain that we are gone."

Elena stared at him, stunned. "Why?"

"They will not allow you to help us. They will kill you, Lena."

"I don't care," she said softly, stubbornly. "I want to help you—all of you. You are my friends, my brothers, my own people."

Fresh pain seemed to enter his gaze, but he did not avert his eyes from her face.

Seeing the conflict that he was in, she continued to beg, "Oh, please, Darren, you must let me help you. You are sick, you are hurt. I want to help."

His eyelids veiled the internal struggle for a time, but then his gaze was determined and his words were strong. "You can help me best by leaving and not coming back. I could not bear it if they did anything to you, Lena."

She blinked back tears, her eyes betraying the inner torture she felt. "Let me stay with you, then. I'd rather die with you than anything else. I've missed you. I even dreamed about you a couple of nights ago."

The man was silent for a moment and then said quietly, a distant tone coming into his voice as if he was standing on the stage once more, addressing the graduating class at their high school, "Consider the path that has been set before you. Do not attempt a journey that is not yours to take. Remain in the place that is best for you."

Exhausted, he bent his back to bear the load once more, a tuft of blond hair falling over his forehead. Then he raised his head and smiled at her, even though he could see that she was silently weeping. "I've missed you, too, Lena. I'm glad you are well. I'll see you again, I'm sure of it."

Elena swallowed hard as she reached out and held him close for one last second. "I'll see you soon, I—I hope—"

"Yes, hope." He nodded, receding back into his distant daydreams, his eyes fixed upon the faraway journey that he had yet to learn. "The hope that keeps us all alive."

She turned quietly and headed back for the staircase. Glancing away from the stretching steps, she saw that Darren was still smiling as he gazed upon the floor, thinking about the wonders that the future would hold.

Elena had no smile upon her face, but her back straightened and her steps became surer as she mounted the path back to the reality of her imprisonment.

CHAPTER EIGHT

Love Out of Place

AS TOLD BY BEKAH WILSON

It was time to go. We understood the danger, but we could not let it stand in our way. We also could not allow time for lengthy goodbyes. Nodding briefly to one another, we set off.

I headed off with the other Americans—two men and a married couple. I caught Sayeed watching me as I swung the pack up on my back. His eyes were always intense, and most of the time it did not bother me, but in this moment of our temporary parting during the mission, I felt timid and could not return his look. I put my back to him and his companions, and we left.

Our job was not that difficult, but it was risky if we were caught. We managed to look like regular tourists ambling through one of the crowded parts of the city. I caught sight of a cloaked woman in blue standing by the doors of a restaurant. She was holding a small child on one hip and a white handkerchief in her free hand. I mumbled something to Katie on my side, but her husband had already seen the woman and turned our group in her direction.

We stopped by the restaurant, pretending to study the menu on the outside of the building. "Salaam," I greeted the woman cautiously and then feigned a sneeze.

"Bless you," she replied under her breath, giving the correct greeting as she shifted the squirming child in her arms and handed me the handkerchief.

I hid my mouth and nose in the cloth and mumbled my correct answer, "Where is your husband?" Then I pretended to sneeze again.

My companions were busily discussing the menu in loud, American voices with an appropriate amount of laughter. It was a straightforward mission and everything was going smoothly. Still, I felt terrified, as if everything could suddenly go wrong in a single moment.

The woman turned and motioned inside the building, yelling something in Arabic, causing me to start. But only a girl appeared, slipping out of the front door with a glass of water and handing it to me. Gratefully, I sat down on the nearby bench, slipping the bag from my shoulder down to my feet. I caught sight of a bearded man standing across the street, but since many people were passing by or idling on the curb, I would not have seen him unless I had been looking.

When I turned aside to hand the glass back to the waiting girl, I knew our mission was complete. I felt welcome relief and looked back toward my friends.

Tom turned at that precise moment and looked at me, smiling kindly. "The humidity get you again? Their food is way too expensive! We'll try closer to the hotel."

His voice was cheerful, light, and optimistic. I smiled back and rose, going to his side, saying something aloud about a touch of headache.

We all turned as one and headed off into the busyness of the street. I felt awkward, as if I had left something undone. I had not thanked the girl for the drink. I had not made eye contact with the man who had taken the bag of forbidden materials and money from right under my nose as planned. I had not said farewell to the woman and her baby. But that is how it was supposed to be. Our mission was complete.

Two hours later, as the sun was going down, we returned to our hotel. I collapsed on the bed in my room, awaiting the arrival of our native friends. I lay there and stared at the ceiling, collecting my thoughts and considering what I would include in the written report.

I thought about the different people we had been informed about and their families. I thought about the restaurant as a cover-up business. I thought about the delicious meal we had just finished eating. Then I thought about Sayeed and sighed.

Sitting up straight, I looked at my phone. It was an hour later than he and his companions were supposed to meet up with us. In fact, they had said they would meet us at the restaurant. I had expressed concern. The others seemed nonchalant. I was the newbie here, and they were experienced veterans. Tom had said I could call him if I wanted to, but he was not concerned. Sayeed was a native, so his time frame was much different than ours.

A knock sounded on the door, and I leapt to my feet, heart all aflutter. Controlling myself, I went to see who it was.

It was Aliya. She smiled at me, her dark eyes shining in her dark face. Every time I saw her, I felt overcome by her beauty. It felt odd, since I saw myself as an average-looking American woman who would never admit to being stunned by another woman's appearance.

"Come in," I murmured, shame welling up in me. I was not romantically attracted to her, or any other woman for that matter, so to even secretly acknowledge her beauty felt wrong. "How did everything go?"

"Very good," she said, her perfect and deeply accented English. "I am very glad to hear that everything went well for you, also."

"Yes, it was fine." I sat down, forcing myself not to feel any tremors, for she had not yet mentioned the rest of her companions. "Did you see anyone downstairs when you came in?"

"Yes." She hesitated, and I felt bewildered by her sudden slowness. Then, in her next words, I understood. "I talked to Tom." She blushed, as much as a dark-skinned woman could.

I smiled at that. "He is a good man." He was indeed a good man, very mild-mannered and kind. He was still in school, so his attention was focused elsewhere, but I imagined one day he would make a good family man.

She caught my eye and laughed under her breath. "Do you mind?" she wondered, a bit of her vulnerable girlishness beginning to show. "I would think—an American man and an American woman, you and he—both of you are on the same mission—"

I laughed a little but not too much, since I did not want to come across as inappropriate for the seriousness of the situation. "I do not mind at all." I motioned her to sit beside me.

Once she complied, I confided, "Tom is a good man, and I do not have any doubts that he would make a good husband. But, no, I am not interested in him at all. And he—I do not think he has ever thought that way toward me, either."

"But why not? I do not understand."

"Maybe our personalities are too much alike," I replied, shrugging. I hesitated when I saw that she still did not understand. After a moment, I decided to be completely honest. "Well, why aren't you attracted to Sayeed? He is from here, like you, and he is also a good man."

Her face gained understanding, and she laughed lightly. "Yes, you are right. It is personality, not where a person is from." Then she looked at me pointedly. "Sayeed loves you."

I looked down, bit my lip, and then raised my eyes to her face again. "Yeah." I did not know what else to say and just felt uneasy. I did not allow myself to act as if I believed her, and at the same time, I did not even know if I wanted to believe her.

"You do not wish for his attention?" Aliya wondered.

Again, I hesitated. "I am afraid to love again. I have been hurt, so my heart is very hard."

She smiled a bit and reached out, putting her hand over mine. "We have all been hurt. But we all still hope for true love."

I nodded, thinking about that. "Yes, you're right," I said after a moment, and then smiled. Perhaps I should be bolder. I thought of Sayeed and his bold words, his dark eyes, and his handsome smile, which was rare but very worth waiting for.

I smiled again and looked back at Aliya. "Where is he?"

"Oh," she replied, appearing surprised. "I do not know. I thought Sayeed came back first. He left us at the station and told us that he would meet us here. He said that he had one more thing to do."

"He didn't come back here—at least, not before you." I sighed, feeling all my nervous energy quickly returning. "I am too impatient, maybe. Tom and the others tell me to relax. How can I relax? I feel so nervous about everything." I lay back on the bed and stared up at the ceiling. "I don't know what to do," I groaned.

Aliya bent over me, her face worried. "Should I call Katie?" That was her question whenever I was caught in a moment of indecision, which made me think that she saw Katie as the American team's problem solver.

"I'm fine," I said, waving her away out of my line of sight. "Yes, I am a little crazy, and not many people see that, but I am fine. I'm just tired and confused about this whole thing. I have felt bad about the mission since this morning. I've felt like something bad was going to happen all day long." I sat up and took a deep breath.

Aliya took my hand. "If you have had this thought since the morning, perhaps it is something. I think you should call Sayeed."

"I can't, not like this." I felt like I was at the end of myself, a feeling that was not unfamiliar, but it did not often manifest itself in front of others.

"Then wait for the feeling to pass, and then call him."

I looked at her. "Why don't you call him?"

"I am not concerned," she replied, shrugging. "Sayeed is always wandering somewhere, gathering information, talking to people—"

Her words trailed off, but I knew what she was thinking, so I completed the thought for her. "Getting into trouble."

Aliya smiled. "Yes, he has that tendency." She picked up my cell phone from the bed and pressed it into my hand. "You call him. I will be back."

I sighed and sat there, slumped over, listening to the door open and shut behind her. I stared at the little TracFone that looked like everyone else's on the team. The natives had their own phones, but we Americans had these identical-looking international TracFones.

I had switched mine with Tom's once to prank him, but the silly man did not even notice. He appeared a bit bewildered to see a picture of a tiger in the middle of the screen when he opened it to call our contact for that day. Yet, it was not until Sayeed motioned to me and said in his smooth tone that Tom had been the victim of a carefully organized plot that my friend realized something was amiss. He had laughed then, and I had felt embarrassed that the dark-eyed man had called me out in front of the whole team.

Pushing the memory aside, I smiled and flipped the phone open. I still was not completely comfortable around Sayeed. He was intense and serious, and I had only seen his humor emerge a couple of times in the past month. He was serious about his humor, too, in the same way that he was serious about his grave moments, and it seemed to me that whatever mood he was in, he was all there. Unlike me, who often hid raging emotions behind a calm expression.

I opened my contact list, found his number, and hit the call button. I swallowed hard and waited, listening as the tone rang once, twice, and then a voice answered.

"Hello, Sayeed?" I said in reply, not certain that I recognized the man on the other end.

A heavily accented voice rambled for a moment. I felt confused as the man identified himself as a police officer, telling me something about Sayeed being arrested for criminal activity.

"I'm sorry, sir, I don't understand," I said after a pause in the explanation, a cold fist clutching my heart. "Sayeed is at your police station?"

"Yes, he is here, in prison."

"Oh, is he okay?" I felt like my question was ignorant, but I did not know what else to ask as my heart pounded in my chest.

"Yes, he is fine, fine, but he is here for criminal mischief and criminal activity. He must stay here until tomorrow, so we will bring him before a judge today and make him answer for his crimes—" He rambled on for some time, suddenly talking about money, and I began to feel even more lost and confused.

I knew it was not worth it to ask for any more details, but before I could stop myself, I asked, "May I talk to Sayeed, sir?"

"No, no, that is not permissible, lady, you must go now, I must go—"

Then I heard loud shouts in the background, and the call was disconnected before I could collect my thoughts. I simply sat there, bewildered and feeling sick.

Not knowing what else to do, I put the phone down and walked out into the lobby. Tom and Aliya were there, talking in low tones, and they turned toward me when they heard the door. Aliya looked a bit embarrassed, but Tom smiled at me.

"I just called Sayeed," I said steadily, ignoring my feelings. "It appears that he is in jail for criminal mischief. The police said they would bring him before a judge soon and keep him until tomorrow."

Tom laughed a bit at that. "Imagine that," he said in wonder and looked down at Aliya. "Déjà vu?"

She smiled and nodded, about to say something, but I was already walking away. I went down the hall, deciding to get a drink or go outside and think in the seclusion of the yard. I needed to do something, anything, to escape the madness of my mind.

Apparently, this had happened before. It was obvious that they had no concerns. I felt guilty for feeling full of panic and for wanting to seclude myself in this small time of trouble that was all too familiar to them but completely new to me.

I went outside and walked away from the buildings toward the desert landscape that stretched along the outskirts of town. Finding a good tree with a nice amount of shade, I collapsed underneath it and leaned against the rough bark.

The night was approaching. It was not safe to be alone out here, especially at night, they told us. Sayeed had instructed all of us in measures of safety and precaution. But I did not care. Was I safe? Was Sayeed safe? Was there any one of us who was safe in this strange and politically unstable country?

Perhaps not. But we were also called to be wise. I rose with a sigh and went back inside the hotel. If I could not sleep, I could read or write, and there was much to think about. We would be leaving in the space of three days and still had much to do. Everything had gone well so far, and our job in the city was completed for this journey. All that was left to do was take as many pictures as possible and write as much information as we could for the outside world.

When I went back inside my room, it was nine o'clock, and they were calling for evening prayers at the mosque. I picked up the phone again and looked at it. On a whim, I called Sayeed's number again. The phone immediately went to voicemail. I had never heard his message before. It was in Arabic, which I was still hardly familiar with, but I could understand the general flow.

"Hello, you have reached Sayeed. Please leave me a message and I will call you back."

It was a normal message, one that people use all over the world regardless of their tongue or nationality. But this one sent shivers through me. His voice was so exotic and beautiful.

The phone beeped, and I did not know what to say. I felt like an idiot.

"Hello, Sayeed," I began in Arabic, and then switched to English, since it was easier to be awkward in my native tongue than in a foreign one. "I hope you are well, and—we're thinking of you, and—" I took a deep breath and ended it all at once, "have a good night, goodbye."

I did not know if others were thinking about him, and I did not care, but since I was, that was all I could think to say. I washed up, got changed, and had no sooner slipped into bed with my favorite notebook and a pen when Aliya came in.

She glanced at me, smiled, and then began changing her clothes.

I knew she was getting ready to go out on an evening date with Tom, and I felt a pang of something that was not jealousy or irritation but felt similar. Let them have their fun, I figured, and perhaps my time would come in the near future.

Sighing, I propped myself up on the pillows and opened my notebook to begin scribbling down whatever I could remember about the day's events. I wrote down the specifics in our prearranged code since it was important to be discreet. But it felt better to write, and I was good at being mysterious.

Aliya emerged from the bathroom in a new dress and began touching up her makeup. I glanced over at her to see her watching me through her mirror.

I felt all business and began asking questions. "How many times has Sayeed been in jail?"

She smiled, as if she knew all along what was on my mind. "I have lost count. I do not even know if he knows!" She laughed quietly and then added, "Life is different here, you know. You can be put in jail for no reason."

"Yeah, I'm realizing that," I replied, scribbling down several additional notes. "Have you ever been arrested?"

"Once, in a group, for being in the wrong place at the wrong time," she admitted. "But we were quickly released, fortunately."

Seeing that she was ready to go, I bid her a good night, not wanting to keep her from spending time with Tom. "Thank you, Aliya. Have a good time."

Her soft voice came back to me from the doorway. "Goodnight, my sister. Sleep well."

I stared out the window, lost in thought for a few moments. It was the fifth mission we had been on, and the first that had a slight complication, but it would be all right.

"Won't it?" I wondered aloud before bending my head over my notebook once more.

Before I knew it, it was morning and I was awake. I rose quickly, feeling impatient for some unknown reason. It was the complete opposite of the previous morning. Yesterday, I had risen reluctantly, feeling a great dread. Today, I was impatient to get up. I was convinced that something was happening without me.

Aliya was still asleep, since it was still early, so I was quiet. I washed and dressed, slipping out of the room without detection. I took a cup of tea, a few pieces of cheese, and some buttered bread in the breakfast room, but I was not that hungry. As the sun rose, I continued to feel more impatient.

It was still quiet downstairs, and it was quiet outside as well. It was still not safe to be alone outside, supposedly, but again, I felt a rebel streak and went into the back courtyard anyway.

It was warm outside but not quite hot, and I knew that as the sun rose higher that it would be another hot and humid day. I returned to my familiar tree and sat beneath it, staring across the barren landscape of dry scrub bushes and rolling rocky hills that led to the villages beyond. I unexpectedly wanted to run and shout and be a general nuisance, but instead, I simply sat still and watched the morning come alive.

An unknown amount of time had already passed when I heard quiet steps in the dusty path behind me. I had a sudden thought of possible danger and wondered if I should rise and flee, but before I could react, a pair of shoes stood beside me. I glanced up quickly to see the calm face of Sayeed standing above me.

I quickly rose, feeling awkward and embarrassed that he had caught me outside after instructing all of us very pointedly not to go anywhere alone. Yet, I felt amazed and delighted to see him alive and well—and free.

He said nothing for a moment, just watching me as the sun continued to rise higher on the horizon. I did not know what to say, feeling flushed and nervous.

After a minute, he suddenly said, "Come, walk with me."

Obediently, I went with him, still feeling nervous.

We walked away from the hotel toward the distant villages, taking our own path among the rocks and sandy shadows. I knew that we were not really going anywhere, so I wondered what he wanted to say to me.

Generally, I did not mind silence, but this time, I felt a mixture of fear, excitement, and the overwhelming need to speak. So, after another minute, I gathered my nerves to ask, "Are you angry with me?"

Sayeed looked down at me, his dark eyes searching mine, a hint of a smile around his mouth, surprise in his tone. "Angry?"

"For being outside, for always escaping, for always trying to be alone—that kind of thing."

"No, I am not angry." When he gave me a genuine smile, I felt reassured and hoped he would keep talking. He walked on, forcing me to follow so I could hear what he was saying.

"I always knew you were a bit of a rebel." He glanced at me again, his mellow voice breaking slightly when he laughed to see how my expression became indignant. "You are a rule follower, yes, but you like time away from the crowd to explore and discover, to be your own person."

I ignored all of that, knowing that he was right and having nothing to say in response. "Why did you end up in jail?" I asked instead.

He sighed. "I am a rebel, too, yes, and the police can sense that, although they do not understand that I use my independence for good instead of for evil."

"But what did you do?"

"Nothing much," Sayeed admitted. "I was walking through the market and stopped a pickpocket from running off with some expensive wares. Since I was with him, the police took me in as well. They searched me and found nothing except for some money, which they found adequate payment, I suppose."

I looked up at him. "I have a hard time believing that they always think that you're a criminal. You don't seem like a criminal at all."

He smiled at me patiently. "I assure you, I do not see it either, but there is something that they see in me that they do not see in others, and they translate it into criminal activity instead of activity for good."

I sighed. "Oh well, I'm glad you're okay anyway. Aliya said it happens a lot, so I guess you're used to it."

"Perhaps I am used to it, but that does not make it pleasant."

I simply nodded in reply, feeling a familiar sense of weariness wash over me. It was the same sensation I experienced during our very first team meeting several months ago when we were back in Washington and listening to our organizers prepare us for our upcoming trip. Hearing about the city's rules and regulations, I felt a sense of hopelessness and wondered how the natives were able to face the injustices of the broken system on a daily basis.

Sayeed was speaking again. To my surprise, it had nothing to do with our current mission or the ongoing events. Instead, he was talking about his childhood, telling a story about how he used to climb up into a fruit tree in his grandparents' yard, eat as much fruit as he could, and then get a terrible bellyache afterward for being so greedy.

"Where is your family now?" I wondered, feeling hesitant, but wanting to know the truth.

"My parents are dead," he said simply. "They were murdered eighteen years ago. I have one sister who is married and three brothers—my older brothers are married with children and my younger brother was also murdered some years ago."

I listened to all of that in a bit of a daze. How different life was here than back at home. It made all my struggles and difficulties look dim and pale. I looked at him and saw him differently. He was a true soldier, having endured much hardship and loss but remaining strong and watchful for others.

We walked on in silence for a moment and then I had to know.

"Do you ever feel angry or bitter toward Americans or Westerners in general?" I asked as we stopped by a large heap of rocks and began to turn back.

He looked at me mildly. "No, why should I?"

"Because they are so stupid. Well, *we* are so stupid. We always try to numb pain instead of dealing with it. We live in such prosperity and we are so—well, whiny. We waste so much time on things that do not matter, and we forget that there are people all around the world who are just struggling to survive."

"It is a matter of perspective," Sayeed said calmly. "I do not have time to think about how other people live. I have many things to do, and yes, there are people who live in great prosperity, but there are others who live in danger of their lives every single moment. Why should I worry or be angry about the lot that I have been given?"

"Yeah, you're right," I said, turning away with a sigh, feeling ashamed. What was I doing here with him? I did not belong. I needed to go back to my fat and prosperous country where at least it made sense to be self-critical because we had the time for that and other cynical habits.

"Rebekah," he said after another moment, his voice firm but kind.

I stopped, feeling different when I heard him use my full name instead of the more familiar Bekah that I introduced myself with.

He stepped around to stand in front of me, looking down at me intently. He did not say anything for a minute, which I was grateful for, because I felt like my mind was spinning again and I could not think. I felt confused and lost and all alone, even though I knew I really was not.

What he finally said, however, surprised me into thinking in a straightforward way again instead of in confusing circles.

"You and your friends are leaving in several days," Sayeed said quietly. "I will miss you, Rebekah."

Suddenly, it made sense. That was why I was upset, too. All my feelings of fear and shame had morphed into a vague sense of confusion, but at the root of it was a general grief and sadness because I felt at home in this foreign city and would miss it when I left. And even though I knew only a little about Sayeed, I felt that I would miss him most of all. We had worked together for a whole month, fighting for innocent people in a hostile land, taking care of one another, looking out for one another, and now, we were to be suddenly parted. It was so hard.

I looked up, tears in my eyes. "So, what are we supposed to do now?"

He smiled and stepped closer, wrapping me up in a strong embrace. It went against all protocol, and I was surprised, but we were both rebels enough to ignore the rules momentarily. I willingly hugged him back, feeling comforted by his unexpected kindness toward me.

It was strange, but in that moment, I no longer felt intimidated by him. He had always been kind and protective toward me, and I had never completely feared him, but his intense personality had kept me nervously at bay until he had almost forced himself past my comfort zone and into my personal space. And now what? He had not yet answered my question.

Then I heard him saying with another chuckle in his voice, "You know, that is one thing that I truly like about you. You are very practical."

But I was shedding silent tears against his shoulder and could not answer.

Sayeed set me back from him and took my hands, looking at me kindly. "I do not know you that well, personally, but I will tell you, Rebekah, I felt love for you the minute I saw you. Do you want to know what I thought?"

I hesitated, pulling my hands away from him to wipe the tears from my eyes. When he took my hands again possessively, I sighed and then shrugged and nodded in assent.

"I thought, 'Here is a beautiful woman who has come all the way from the other side of the world to help others who suffer.' And it did not make sense to me why you had come. Not many women come here, and when they do come, they are married. Or occasionally, women will come to look for a husband and take them away to a safer country."

I laughed at that, the very idea sounding ridiculous.

"I am serious," he said, smiling.

"I know, I'm sorry."

"Do not be sorry, but it did not make sense to me," Sayeed said kindly. "But I decided that if there was one thing that I would ask you, it would be this: 'Why have you come? Why are you here?' Certainly, I learned a little bit about you over the weeks. I heard you talking as you worked with your friends, but I wanted to hear it from you."

He continued to look at me intently and held my hands a bit tighter. "So, tell me, beautiful woman, why have you come to this strange and foreign land?"

"I don't know," I replied honestly, flushing under his compliments. "I worked with Tom over the summer, and he and some friends of his were coming here to help and asked for more people to go on their team. I had the money and the time to travel, so it was kind of a spur-of-the-moment decision. I guess everything just fell into place and worked out."

"Indeed, it did," Sayeed said. "And was it hard for you to come?"

"Not as hard as I expected," I admitted. "The people are very nice here, a lot nicer than where I came from. I don't know the language, but a lot of people speak English here, and I had the experience of the team to rely on, so it wasn't that bad."

He continued to watch me and then smiled a bit. "But you were just criticizing your own people for not understanding the difficulties that we have to go through. You seem to understand many things."

I shrugged, feeling the familiar sense of resigned hopelessness. "I saw for myself the huge difference between reality and propaganda—what my country says about your country and what your people actually go through every day suffering under your leaders." I looked up at Sayeed. "At least, you and your people are innocent of your political problems, since you never chose your leaders in the first place."

He simply listened, and I wondered if he could even fathom what I was trying to say. As we walked on, I had the idea that he did know more than I realized, even though I felt like I was an exotic bird visiting his cage and trying to explain freedom to someone who had been born into a prison and could only imagine what it was like to fly free.

Then, before I could think of anything else to say, we were back at the hotel. I did not know what to do. I was struggling internally, and I imagined that he was, as well. When he did not say anything at first, I looked at him and swallowed hard. He was gazing at me, as usual, with a hint of sadness in his eyes.

"I wanted to thank you for being very kind to me and looking out for me while all of us were here," I said honestly. "I know that you looked out for me more than the others, sometimes even when I wandered off. I hope I wasn't too rebellious."

Sayeed smiled slightly. "It was my pleasure to watch out for you, Rebekah. I am happy that no harm ever came to you, for I would have ended up back in prison on your behalf."

I felt surprised and looked up at him questioningly, but he was completely serious. He really and truly did love me. It made me feel special, but also sad, since I knew that I could not love him back. Everything was just too impossible.

"You do not believe me?" he wondered, seeing my searching glance.

"I believe you," I said mildly, turning aside, but my next words were a bit caustic. "I'm glad for your sake that nothing happened, since I don't want to be the cause of anyone's imprisonment."

Sayeed extended his hand to stop me from leaving his side and then said sincerely, "I will miss you, and if you ever return, I will be very glad of it."

His kindness cut through my armor and brought me back from my sadness. I hesitated, wanting to be honest but not sure how to put it. Looking up at him, I tried.

"It's funny, I always felt like you were kind of scary and distant because you were so serious and stared at me all the time without saying much unless it was business, but you are not really scary at all." I laughed at myself, certain that I was stammering and making a fool out of myself. Plus, I felt sad again, for as soon as this friendship had started, it was about to be ended. I wanted to cry freely, the tears burning in the back of my throat and underneath my eyelids.

"I love you," Sayeed told me then, his voice low and husky from his own unshed tears, and I knew he meant it.

I realized suddenly that I loved him, too. I did not know how to tell him, and I knew that I could not speak without bursting into tears, but I nodded and reached out to squeeze his hand.

We parted then, since he was saying, "I must go. There are some friends who need help this morning."

I nodded again, unable to talk and feeling a few uninvited tears trailing down my cheeks.

Sayeed murmured some words to me in his own tongue, which were completely lost on me, but I managed to say some words of farewell before he gave me one last dark-eyed look and turned to walk away around the corner of the building.

I took a moment to collect my thoughts and control my feelings. At last, I went back inside, still conflicted by my strange mix of emotions but feeling contented that we had broken the strange barrier that had lasted between us since the very first day I had invaded his world.

Taking a deep breath, I walked into the lobby and found part of my team sitting around a few tables. They were all, of course, silent, and to the stranger's eyes, it looked like a bunch of jet-lagged foreigners trying to get some caffeine into their veins to function correctly during the day.

Walking over to the table, I sat down wearily. Several glanced up, and the others took their time noticing me.

"You all right?" Tom wondered, seeing my red-rimmed eyes.

"Yes," I said quietly. "I was talking to Sayeed. He came back early this morning and headed off to another quarter to help some friends."

He nodded in understanding. Meanwhile, Aliya was sitting at a nearby table, but I watched their eyes meet momentarily and knew that they understood.

For appearance's sake, none of us could be together in public, so I wondered what all of this meant for the future. Was the love the four of us felt strong enough to withstand the barriers of time zones, countries, political unrest, social prejudices, and more?

Only time would tell. That was the real hope we clung to.

Two short mornings later, the team was assembled and ready to depart back to our own world. I rose with a sigh from the couch in the lobby to mumble something about bringing my bag downstairs. I was the last straggler. It was kind of everyone to wait.

I felt broken as I went upstairs and scanned my card in the lock for the last time. After double-checking the room for any last belongings, I zipped up my bag and paused to stare out the window that overlooked the city.

"Goodbye, Sayeed, until we meet again," I whispered with some sadness, knowing his busy schedule of helping others prevented him from seeing us off. Plus, who knew when we would ever cross paths again—or if we were destined to part ways forever?

As sad as I felt, I was also grateful for the things that I had learned—about life, about love, about my new friends on the other side of the world, and about the possibilities for the future.

I shouldered my bag and glanced at the clock. It was time to go.

CHAPTER NINE

My One True Love

AS TOLD BY SAM KRITZER

I can't rightly say when my one true love first came into my life. Technically, yes, I can tell you the exact day and a good estimate of the time when I first saw her, but for me, she seemed to exist long before then.

The date was April 25, a Thursday, and it had been a long day at work. I was tired but not ready to go home. I was not looking forward to facing the noise, the smell, and the drama of my apartment complex, so I decided to take a few moments to relax and breathe on my own.

I walked into that coffee shop on the corner. You know, the one that everyone went to before work, after work, at lunch, at break time, and whenever else they had an excuse to grab a cup of joe and rest their feet a bit. Well, I went in there and sat down away from all the people, leaning back in a chair and not really caring about the rest of the world.

I wasn't in the mood for coffee. In fact, I had been thinking about hitting the bar instead, but I wanted to be left alone. The last few times I went to my favorite bar to try and relax, I had to suffer through nosy questions and dull conversation, so it was fast falling out of my list of places to hang out.

After a few minutes, I did get to buy a cup of coffee, but I didn't intend to drink it. It was just an excuse so I could stay there a few minutes longer and forget about the responsibilities and pressures of life for a bit. There was always too much to do.

I just sat there, staring aimlessly out the window. Everything was blurred in the dirty glass, and it looked good that way. The mood I was in, my mind was blurred, so it seemed natural for the rest of the world to stay foggy and dim, faraway and distant.

After a few minutes and a few sips of coffee, I felt better. It was nice to be alone, after a whole day of rushing around with this meeting, that person to talk to, this call to take, that report to take care of. But my heaviness lingered, which made me wonder. I felt—strange.

You ever get that feeling of complete loneliness when in a crowd of people? That was part of what I felt, sitting in the coffee shop, surrounded by busy people in a rushed world. I closed my eyes for a moment and felt it even stronger. I opened my eyes and looked around, searching for more insight.

As I looked through the glass again, I could only see my confused reflection looking back at me. Even I looked blurred.

Another man who was a bit older than me also showed up in the glass. He was sitting at the table next to mine and reading a paper, appearing to be happily oblivious to my probing examination.

I felt a peculiar sensation, different than the original loneliness. I wasn't sure what it was, though I know now, but as my gaze continued to be drawn to the glass, I found another pair of eyes. Lonely and searching eyes, like mine, but different.

I looked for those eyes and the blurred face they belonged to in the coffee shop. The man at the table next to me was blocking them, so I moved my chair back a bit—and froze.

The eyes were still looking out the window, but they were real and not just a blurred image in the streaked glass. They belonged to a pretty face, the prettiest face I had seen in a long time. At that recognition, my heart leapt. I knew exactly why I had felt strangely restless. It was her, the one and only.

She was just sitting there, her chin resting on her palm with her elbow on the table and her other hand clasping her propped-up elbow. She gazed out the window, as if in a daydream.

I continued to stare at her, wishing she would do something instead of sit there like a statue. I considered approaching and offering to buy her a coffee. Her table was empty, after all. But I did not want to interrupt. She looked so perfect and calm in this crazy world, quite out of place.

There—she moved. She fidgeted slightly in her seat, as if uncomfortable, and then put her hands down on the table, glancing around suspiciously, as if someone had pinched her and she was looking for the culprit. Seeing nothing in her vicinity, she seemed to relax a bit. I continued to watch in fascination as she continued to search, her eyes slowly traveling around the room, briefly examining every person in the shop.

Her eyes suddenly rested upon me without warning. Now I was the one who couldn't move. Her bright green eyes widened as if surprised, but there was no fear, only curiosity. She had discovered the culprit, and now she was wondering why I was still staring.

I wanted her to gaze at me like that forever. But I couldn't help myself and accidentally spoiled the moment. I felt my ears burning hot, and I dropped my eyes. Just for a second, but something changed in that moment.

After I composed myself and looked back, I found a laughing smile on her face. She was so pretty, so charming—bright green eyes, long curly red hair framing her soft cheeks, a cute nose, and such sweet lips. I just had to smile back, even as I could feel the heat spreading from my ears to the rest of my face.

Then she was the one to turn away, and I could see color rising in her cheeks and the slight droop to her eyelids, showing that she recognized my interest and was not devoid of any feeling herself. I wanted to get up and meet her, ask her name, and maybe get her number if I was lucky. But I felt rooted in my spot and could not move.

She fidgeted in her seat again, this time pulling her cell phone from her pocket and holding it to her ear. I followed her movements closely, watching her through the smudged glass. When she began to look unhappy, I clenched my jaw and mentally cursed whoever called her. There was a droop to her shoulders now, and her eyes looked distant through the glass.

Presently, she pulled the phone away from her ear and pushed her chair away from the table, rising swiftly now. I watched in fascination as she began to collect her belongings, things scattered about the table that I did not even notice previously—a notebook, pens, extra paper, a book, to name a few. She was all aflutter now, packing up her oversized purse and getting ready to go.

I gulped hard as she pushed the chair back into the table and the realization hit me. She was leaving. She would be gone, out of my life as quickly as she entered it. I had to do something.

Awkwardly, I got up and staggered after her, hoping to catch her before she reached the door. But no, she was too fast, headed for the parking lot without a backward glance.

I grabbed at the door and shoved my way out, searching. She couldn't be far.

No, there she was, walking up next to a car parked only a few spaces from my own truck. Too bad. I wished she didn't have a car. I wished a tire had blown. I wished she had run out of gas. I wished—I do not remember what else I wished. If only she did not have a car! I could have been the lucky fellow to drive her home.

I had to talk to her before she drove away. I had to say something. I swallowed hard, feeling nervous, not knowing what to do or what to say.

Time was of the essence, so I forced my legs to move forward and keep going. She was standing by the driver's door now and had her keys out. I was nearer now, next to her car. I stopped, seeing that my shadow fell across her car and that she had paused to turn toward me, the intruder.

Now quite near her, I was surprised to see how small she was. She was so small that the top of her head just about reached my shoulder and she had to tilt her head back to look straight at me. At a distance, I had seen her as larger than life. Nearby, even though she was physically small, I could distinctly feel the weakness of my humanity and wondered if she was of earthly substance or not.

She continued to stand still, watching my face. Her eyes were wide and questioning, but there was no fear. Still, I wanted to somehow assure her of my good intentions. I had to say something, just to break the tension.

If I could only summon my voice from wherever it disappeared to. I swallowed hard, the lump in my throat refusing to leave. I could have extended my hand in greeting, but I was not interested in a business transaction. Besides, my hands were so clammy that I dared not draw attention to them.

If I could only talk, I was sure she would understand and that she would respond. She seemed like a friendly girl, and I was sure I could reassure her that I was also friendly. But I had to say something, so I forced my mouth open.

"Hi, I'm Sam."

CHAPTER TEN

Faithless Friends and Replacement Lovers

On an otherwise ordinary Tuesday evening toward the end of summer, Connie McCalister came home from work to find an invitation sitting in the mailbox, stuck between a couple of pieces of junk mail. The official-looking cream-colored envelope caught her attention, but it was the out-of-state address and the seal on the back that gave her momentary pause. When was the last time she had been to her alma mater in Boston?

Standing in the kitchen several minutes later, Connie allowed the memories to wash over her, but then she tossed the envelope on the table and turned away to her bedroom to change before starting dinner. Her roommate, Mackenzie Stewart, would be home in about half an hour, and she would be hungry.

Later that night, Connie stood in her room before her desk to stare at the envelope one last time before getting ready for bed. When she finally opened it during supper at Mac's insistence, she found a notice from the alumni association inviting her to the next class reunion.

Connie turned from the desk and went to the window, pulling away the curtain and staring out into the dark night. She could see her reflection in the window pane and realized that she did not look that much different from when she was back in her old college days. Even though the past ten years had changed her in many ways, she still felt largely the same open curiosity about her future.

Then again, not that she was overly sentimental, but college always brought back a lot of harsh memories. Perhaps most people could muscle through their mixed feelings about the past, and usually she did just that, but for the moment, she allowed herself to remember the faces of those who hurt her the most and consider the what-ifs.

"You should go," Mac told Connie the next morning in her usual blunt fashion as she packed a lunch for the day.

Connie stood at the sink, washing the breakfast dishes with a smirk on her face. "Want to come along? You ever been to Boston in the fall?"

"No, thank you," Mac said sarcastically and then began talking about her work schedule for the next two months. Soon, she was picking up her jacket and keys and heading out the door.

"Have a good day," Connie murmured as she finished drying the silverware. A couple of minutes later, she was also on her way out the door. As Connie cast a glance at the calendar on the fridge, she decided to put the matter of the invitation out of mind until the RSVP deadline.

A month and a half later, Connie found herself with a hotel reservation on the outskirts of the City of Boston. She had taken a half-day from work to drive out there and arrived with several hours to spare before the dinner party. After settling into her room, she threw herself on the big bed for a bit of rest, taking the time to check her email and catch up on a few texts.

Once she had nothing else with which to distract herself, she simply lay there, lost in thought. She already felt nervous about the evening's ordeal and the possibility of coming face-to-face with certain people from her past. Yet, as the time drew closer, Connie told herself that it was not a big deal to participate in all the hoopla and rose to shower and dress for the occasion without further consideration.

An hour later, Connie walked into the expansive lobby of the main campus building and immediately spotted the primary object of all of her nervousness—Tracy Williams. Her hair was a different color, she looked thinner and frailer than ever before, and she had since married and changed her last name to O'Donnell, but she was the same Tracy that Connie always remembered. She was turned away slightly, standing next to her husband Ron while chatting up another couple with enthusiasm as if she did not have a care in the world.

Connie stopped staring and moved on, realizing she would always remember Tracy the same way—frail and flighty but always the life of the party, able to pass out friendly enthusiasm to everyone who crossed her path. Connie wondered if she would always view herself in the opposite manner—quiet and steady but always on the outside looking in, never able to connect with the people she so greatly admired.

Before she could get lost in thought, Connie ran into Scott Emerson, his wife Amy, and their little blond-haired boy. She chatted with them for a few moments, reminiscing with Scott about physics class and telling Amy about the time he had been tempted to steal her answers instead of potentially embarrassing himself by asking the professor for help.

Both Scott and Amy laughed at that memory, and while that brief conversation was more funny than serious, Connie felt much better.

"Have you seen Sue?" Scott broke into her thoughts, just as they were about to head in different directions.

Before Connie had a chance to answer, there was Sue, all smiles and an extra few pounds to boot. Her hug was just as warm as ever, and she held on for an extra few seconds. Next thing Connie knew, Sue was dragging her over to a corner table where the room was quieter, putting a drink in her hand, and asking her directly if she had seen Tracy, Ron, Maria, Jimmy, Andi, or Marcus.

"I saw Tracy," Connie said in a bland tone, looking away from Sue's pointed stare. Instead, her eyes drifted, almost against her will, to the spot where she had last seen her old friend. Tracy was still there, now watching from the other side of the room. Connie hurriedly turned away and a momentary stab of grief cut through her embarrassment, leaving her cheeks flushed.

"Actually," she whispered to Sue, "Tracy is looking this way right now."

Sue cursed freely under her breath and moved her chair a bit so as not to allow herself to look in the same direction. Connie felt another stab of grief, but this time she wanted to say something to defend Tracy from Sue's curse.

Glancing back at Tracy, Connie saw the woman toss her head in her characteristic way and laugh as she said something to another friend. So, Connie bit her tongue and looked directly at Sue, who was busily rattling off a lot of gossip about Tracy's husband, who apparently had quite the reputation.

When Sue took a breath, Connie quickly asked, "What have you been up to recently?"

Then came another whirlwind story about work drama, family drama, husband drama, in-law drama, and whatever other drama Sue could conjure up at the moment.

By the time Sue took another breath, the two of them were seated for dinner and surrounded by many other colleagues who were rather distinguished by this point in their lives. It was good food for the most part, but Connie was already beginning to tire of the drama of the company, so her mind began to drift to other things in her life.

Connie woke up slightly at the end of the meal, just before dessert was served, to see several colleagues rising to give speeches. Who should be the second person to the podium but old Jimmy Becker, Connie's ex from senior year.

"Oh wow," Connie murmured under her breath, seeing him walk up to the podium with the same self-assured, attention-grabbing manner he always wore.

Sue glanced at her, puzzled to hear amazement in her voice.

"There's one that did not age gracefully!" Connie whispered in some consternation, but then she kept her lips firmly closed, since she knew Sue had always greatly admired Jimmy for his brains and his charisma, even if his looks had since deteriorated.

Here was Jimmy, sporting a graying mustachio and at least an extra 50 pounds since graduation. He sounded the same as ever—smart, intriguing, pompous, condescending. He spoke about how the corporate world was being affected by artistry, which was a curious concept, but not riveting to Connie, so she had a hard time concentrating on the speech.

When everyone stood to applaud, Connie glanced at Sue to see her sigh with happiness. Once again, she resolved to keep her mouth shut at the risk of coming across as spiteful and mean. No sooner had Connie so decided, they sat down to dessert and Sue began to relate Jimmy's personal life of the past several years—a sudden marriage, a messy divorce, some years of freewheeling, and then another sudden marriage.

"I thought for years that he was making the wrong decision," Sue told Connie, looking at her in a meaningful way that Connie purposefully ignored, "but Ginny seems really sweet, so hopefully everything will work out."

Tired of the gossip, the talks, the low murmur of voices that created a dull roar in her head, Connie endured the last speech in which several alumni spoke of institutional funding and the hope to continue future meetings, dinners, and get-togethers. Of course, President Bob Gingham, ever-present in alumni manners, encouraged everyone to attend the great line-up of talks scheduled for Saturday morning.

"Will you be there tomorrow?" Sue asked as they rose to join the guided campus tour and check out the latest improvements.

"No, thank you," Connie replied in a non-committal way, never having been interested in campus politics. "I'll look up the meeting notes if I'm interested."

"Well, how about coming to another gathering?" Sue urged.

Connie shrugged. "Probably not, but if you are ever in Connecticut, by all means, please look me up."

Sue laughed a bit, but then caught sight of Joe and Terra, some other friends of hers. With a quick hug and a smooch on the cheek, Connie found herself relieved of Sue.

Connie slipped away from the crowds, deciding to take her own tour of the main building, walk around campus a little, and then sign out for the night. There was a free campus concert in the auditorium by a band she knew little about, but after hanging out in the back for several minutes, she moved on, not in the mood to listen to loud music.

Happy to be alone for a little while, Connie strolled about and thought about the past and the present. Seeing everyone brought back memories, but she had no regrets. In fact, the more she encountered people from her past, the happier she felt about her present life.

Catching a glimpse of herself in the big glass windows on one side of the building she was walking through, she sighed and shook her head. How was it that so many of her friends had gained so much weight and aged so terribly? She certainly did not understand, for she had taken no special efforts to maintain her own youthful appearance. While her looks were by no means of the ultimate importance, Connie wondered if it was a greater demonstration of how disciplined she lived in comparison to most people in the world.

A half-hour later, after a quiet stroll around the premises and a few brief chats with some others, Connie found herself on the upper deck of the rec building, staring out into the cool and dark night and feeling happy to be alone once again. She unexpectedly thought of the time she stood up there alone, shortly after Jimmy had broken up with her in the little coffee shop around the corner. His words had cut her like a knife that windy day when he decided that their lives were going in different directions.

It was an odd time for such a particular memory, since she cared little for Jimmy now and felt no animosity toward him, neither when he had given his pompous speech, nor when they had briefly greeted each other several minutes ago. In fact, when they had bumped into each other in the hallway, Jimmy had been the one to look surprised to see Connie, but he had always been bad at hiding his feelings.

His wife, a pretty woman who matched him in size and structure, looked Connie up and down critically and then treated her just as condescendingly as her husband did.

Connie had not allowed their arrogant stares to make her feel awkward, but then Jimmy had said to her in a pompous tone, "Well, if it isn't Constant Connie McCalister! I guess you still look the same as ever."

She had smiled slightly and nodded her head, acknowledging the old college nickname, but now she wondered what type of constancy she was known for and what constancy of appearance had to do with it.

Perhaps Jimmy was referring to the time when he told her, "You have always looked extraordinarily pretty with the innocence of a child, which is quite preferable to glamorous beauty any day." They had been dating for only a month at the time, and she had laughed freely, considering his words pure flattery.

Or perhaps Jimmy was thinking of the time he had cruelly said, "I could never be long-term with such a simpleton—and the looks to match."

Connie decided that even if she did not fully understand what sort of constancy she was known for, Jimmy had certainly remained constant in his attitude toward her. Even though she had forgiven him for his cruelty toward her, the memory still stung a bit. Yet, since it was a stinging thought, it was only a sting and then it was over. Connie knew that it was a false and an ignorant thing for him to say, and she needed no human being to affirm her in the truth of who she was.

The memory that genuinely ached was when Tracy's green eyes settled on Connie from across the room that evening. She thought of all they had shared from years ago, which they had suddenly and strangely lost. The pain of loving and losing lovers was almost expected at one point or another, but the cruelty of faithless friends was a completely different thing to comprehend.

"And woe to the person who has a lover as a faithless friend," Connie murmured to herself, feeling fortunate that she had never come to that point with Jimmy and had never experienced that type of hurt. She imagined that type of grief would be unbearable.

Hearing the sliding door behind her squeak, Connie glanced around to see Tracy slipping out of the rec lounge and coming across the deck toward her. Connie stood stock still, nearly holding her breath and almost afraid that if she said anything, she would frighten Tracy away. She had no idea if Tracy actually was afraid of her, but she often had imagined that such was the case because of how suddenly the break in their relationship had happened without a clue of what had occurred. It was almost as if Tracy had died without the closure of a funeral.

Tracy looked at Connie now, plainly, but it was not an open gaze. Tracy's eyes were more veiled now, for they were not as clear as they had once seemed to Connie. Before Connie could dismiss her own shocked daze and summon her courage to say hello, Tracy was talking.

All her showy behavior, all her laughter, all her carefree bravado that Tracy gave to the whole wide world was gone.

She was simply the girl that Connie had once known and loved.

But Tracy was different now. She had changed. She was talking about her husband and their blonde-haired daughter and their son with a southern name, and her parents, and his parents, and their different work schedules and responsibilities—it was plain and matter-of-fact without the flair and exuberance that Sue's gossip provided.

Connie felt sadness for Tracy quietly creeping in to replace her initial surprise. Beneath all the plain and stark details of her life, Connie could hear Tracy's simple cry for help.

But at that instance, Tracy stopped talking about herself and looked pained. Controlling herself, she forced a smile and then asked, "Did you see—did you talk to Jimmy?" She caught herself halfway, remembering that they had all seen him give a speech at dinner.

"I said hello to him and his wife," Connie said calmly, her eyes never leaving Tracy's.

Tracy's green eyes flashed slightly and she gazed greedily at Connie, almost desperate for some sign of inner emotion. "What did you—what was it like to see him again?"

Connie shrugged slightly at that, baffled at why Tracy would ask, confused why Tracy would suddenly care how she was doing now. Yes, Tracy had always been there for her, but then again, Tracy had walked away when her own life began to be a bit difficult.

Almost casually, Connie answered, "It's obvious to me that Jimmy chose his own path—the famous, popular life that he always wanted. I hold nothing against him for that. In fact, I have no regrets. I am enjoying the quiet life that I prefer, and I'm glad he found what he was looking for all along." When Tracy remained silent for a moment, Connie added, "A lot of people choose different paths, you know?"

"Yes," Tracy said slowly, searching her former friend's face.

Connie gazed back evenly, but her defenses were up and she knew that she, at least, would never be able to trust Tracy as she once had unless there was a major shift. Tracy had always had a deep and perceptive intuition about people, so Connie could sense that Tracy knew that she was not going to willingly open up without some demonstration of good faith. After all, Connie had been the one to call and leave unanswered messages. She had been the one to wait days, weeks, months, even years on end. The next move was Tracy's.

Tracy finally did break the silence. "Yes, a lot of people choose a different path from the one they first expected to walk." She was gazing past Connie as she spoke, but the green eyes flitted back again momentarily. "I envy you sometimes," she admitted, and then, just like that, she was gone.

Connie stood still in stunned silence, feeling confusion surround her like a fog. How was she enviable of all people? It was not that Connie did not like herself or the course of her life, but she failed to see what part of her life was envied by others. Did they envy the pain they caused her? Or the way that Connie was constantly polite and kind in the face of rude and unkind actions from others? What exactly was it?

Connie thought about it the rest of the evening and throughout the night, but doubted that real answers even existed for the kind of questions that she had about life. For all their fancy college education, what had her graduating class really learned about relating to one another?

The following day, Connie was happy to return home and was looking forward to catching up with her roommate. But Mac did not get home until late that Saturday, and she slept in on Sunday morning, so Connie did not get a chance to talk to her until Sunday afternoon.

Mac was full of news, and Connie was especially relieved not to have to talk about her weekend adventures immediately.

But after her words were spent, Mac looked at Connie pointedly. "So, was it that bad?"

Connie sighed a bit, leaning back in her chair and feeling a bit annoyed that Mac assumed that much about her. Yet, she also knew that her roommate would not add to whatever hurt she might have experienced over the weekend.

"They're doing a nice bunch of improvements on the campus buildings," Connie said shortly. "The dinner was nice, and I saw a bunch of old friends and enemies. It was interesting, but I'm glad to be done with that chapter of life, and I didn't go to all the alumni meetings because you know how bored I get at meetings."

"Yeah," Mac said, rolling her eyes slightly, being one who greatly enjoyed meetings of every sort. "But what's this about enemies? I didn't know that you had any!"

Connie laughed a bit. "Well, not really enemies in the strictest sense. Old ex-friends, I guess you could say. My ex Jimmy looks old and fat, and his new wife does too. Then there's my old best friend Tracy, who looks sad and haggard. I was shocked at how out of shape a lot of people looked. Even my gal Sue, who used to be into all these diets and work-out regimens, looks kind of bloated and processed."

"That sucks," Mac said plainly.

"Yeah," Connie admitted, "but such is life. We all have to deal with faithless friends now and then. The point, however, is to remain faithful and disciplined regardless of how others are."

Mac gave a noncommittal grunt in agreement and reached for her phone. "That's why they call you Constant Connie. Just make sure you aren't constantly being trampled on, kid."

Connie shrugged. "I'd rather constantly be trampled on than be as mean and fat as some."

"Well," Mac said after a moment, putting down her phone. "How about some cheese for your wine?"

"I'm quite content, thank you," Connie said in her loftiest tone.

Mac laughed. "I'm actually going to get some ice cream." She rose and disappeared into the kitchen.

Connie leaned back comfortably and began to reflect on life, but then she remembered that Mac rarely ate ice cream. In fact, neither of them did, and they never kept it in the house. The only time they had ice cream was when one of Mac's friends came over and brought a carton or two with him.

This friend, who Mac adamantly insisted was nothing more than an actual friend, would occasionally come over and talk with Mac for hours about all sorts of things, sitting at the kitchen table with her to chat, even after Connie went to bed.

Connie smiled at that realization, glad for the distraction from her morbid thoughts about the people she knew from her past. Grant was a good guy. Maybe they all didn't have to be faithless and pompous jerks.

"Hey!" she called around the corner into the kitchen. "If it's chocolate, bring me some, too!"

Chapter Eleven

Sweet Vengeance

The woman's name was Madeline Barker. Once upon a time in high school, her youthful face had been framed with very straight, medium-long, strawberry blonde hair, producing envy in all the girls and adoration among all the boys. Now, decades later, her fair locks had been sacrificed upon the altar of the light ash blonde permanent wave.

Now, Madeline primped her bangs in her hand mirror for the umpteenth time that day and replaced the object in her desk drawer. Today was a bad hair day for certain, but it provided a most pleasant excuse to temporarily escape from the copious amount of letters scattered across her disorganized desk.

With an effort, she turned her swivel chair around and once more surveyed the damage of the afternoon mailman's visit. Ugly lines appeared on her forehead, which she smoothed out with effort, but they immediately sprang out again, as if they had a mind of their own and were quite undecided on their current course of action.

Madeline blamed the crease lines on her divorce five years ago. She blamed them on the death of her second husband two years ago. She blamed them on her thirty-year-old daughter's marriage to a forty-year-old woman just last month. She blamed them most of all on her current occupation, certain that if she retired, the aging process would be happily reversed.

At the beginning of every New Year, Madeline swore she would retire from the desk job that had held her in bondage for fourteen years. She had said as much for over three years now, but the pay was fair and the work was easy, so it was difficult for her to choose another course of action.

Picking up the first envelope within reach, she noted the date stamp read April 23, several weeks past the official start of the second quarter. Frowning again with the assistance of her accursed wrinkles, Madeline tore the missive open and glanced over the contents of the two pages.

It was the same old story day in and day out. One person was unhappy with their current insurance policy, another wished to renew but was unable to find all of the corresponding paperwork, and yet another was resentfully following through with their recurring payment but wished to do business with a more reasonable company. One thing was for certain—if her customers were unhappy, her boss would be mighty displeased, and she certainly couldn't let that happen.

"It's a thankless job," Madeline had admitted to her friends over bridge last Wednesday evening.

As always, they responded with awe and praise. "You're braver than most!" "God bless you!" "More power to you!" And her least favorite, "Better you than me!"

The last comment was always ominously pronounced by Emily Ruckstein, a frail woman of Madeline's own age whom she had first met in sixth grade. While their youthful friendship began satisfactorily enough, the most pervasive element of their relationship was competition—in the school plays, at the high school prom, in the cheerleading group, and even where boyfriends were concerned.

As she stabbed the letter opener into the corner of a delicate cream envelope, Madeline envisioned an ugly scar slowly beginning to form across Emily's fair and unblemished face.

"Botox," she muttered spitefully, though she held a nagging suspicion that her assumptions were false. "It has to be that—or the constant escapades to Bermuda, Costa Rica, Mexico, and the Keys," she said aloud, in an effort to comfort herself.

After all, it was not her fault that she had married poor while Emily had won the hand of the richest boy in their class. Handsome Bobby Ruckstein. It was only a blind girl who did not at least once swoon over that tall young man with the hair that shone like ripe wheat in the afternoon sun. Indeed, the brilliance of his flashing copper eyes incited great emotions in all females, and least of all because of the shiny new pennies sparkling in his pockets.

Surveying the return address that hailed from New York City, Madeline remembered the newly engaged 19-year-old Emily and the happy glow on her wan face as she described the new apartment they would move into after their honeymoon. Those forty-odd years felt like yesterday, creating a new crease in her forehead as she realized there was no hope for her happiness in this life. Her most hopeful chance of living pleasantly was to retire within five years and find a cleaner apartment closer to the town where her son resided.

The jangling phone interrupted her dismal memories. She allowed it to ring twice more, then swiftly picked it up and begrudgingly blurted the company name into the receiver. Listening to the elderly woman on the other end inquiring about her options for dealing with a missed application deadline, Madeline realized that Emily Ruckstein had finally blundered for once in her life. A customer could certainly correct filing the wrong paperwork or right the accidental false information written therein, but Hardy's Insurance never *ever* missed a deadline.

Madeline silently gloated as the woman continued describing her plight. At last, it was her chance to feel the deep satisfaction of sweet revenge she had been waiting for since her younger days.

When the silence echoed on the other end of the line, Madeline straightened in her chair and jutted out her chin. A wave of self-righteousness and a sense of justice thrilled her to the depths of her very soul.

"That is not my problem, ma'am," she said calmly, adding the respectful title as an afterthought, hoping to show her absence of hard feelings. "The state simply does not allow our insurance customers to miss deadlines."

The disappointed woman was momentarily at a loss. At last, she quietly admitted her fault and politely ended the call.

Banishing the bitter wrinkles with a benevolent smile, Madeline primly turned back to the letters, opening each with a flourish and setting them aside in neat piles according to their contents. At last, at long last, her rival had been bested.

Hearing a step in the hall, the aged brown head was raised and the amber eyes rested on an old man shuffling through the doorway. Her brows came together with an irritated scowl as she realized that he was about to interrupt her peace. Then Madeline remembered her accomplishment of only several minutes previous and silently gloated once more. Sitting upright once more, she motioned to the chair in front of her desk with a delicate wave of her shapeless hand.

"Hullo, dear," the elderly man croaked, grinning at her toothlessly as he pulled a creased and begrimed packet of papers from his tattered brown coat. "I come back, you see. I remembered."

"So you did," returned Madeline, dryly, her words betraying her gentle actions. "Did you bring back *everything* this time? I'm still holding your application, you know. The state won't wait much longer, or I'll get in trouble."

"Yep, I b'lieve I got it." Unfolding the packet, he leaned forward and brushed her mail aside, smoothing the papers out on the desk. Looking at her, the nut-brown face beamed the familiar toothless grin. "Ev'rythin' good?"

"Very good," the woman murmured after a hasty glance over the paperwork. "You are an old dear, that you are." Managing a smile, Madeline gingerly lifted the packet from the desk and ceremoniously paper-clipped it to several sheets lying nearby. "I'll just take care of that this afternoon, and you'll be all set," she concluded, setting it down once more with a flourish.

"Good, good." He sat there a moment longer, still grinning at her.

Madeline eyed him and then smiled back as he slowly rose and headed for the door. She was still thinking about Emily's great blunder with great satisfaction. Then, suddenly, her bliss increased upon the realization that the exiting poor old pensioner was a perfect match for her old rival.

Emily Shaw, indeed. While such a name was rather boring and plain, the dullness of it brought absolute delight to her imagination.

With the old man out of earshot, the woman allowed herself one indelicate sigh. With Emily Shaw safely out of the way, she could once more resort to being Madeline Ruckstein. The very name was music to her ears. She smiled, thinking how pleased Bob would be to have her as a wife. For once, he would not need to worry about providing a thin, sickly, pale woman with health coverage and frequent visits to warmer climates. Instead, he could pamper his healthy, robust, and highly capable wife with luxurious vacations to Europe or the faraway tropical islands.

"Dear old Bob Ruckstein," Madeline murmured, shaking her head as she bent over the letters once more. Her mind drifted to the last time she saw him. He was still tall and still handsome, and though his hair had turned gray and his coppery eyes were now rheumy, he was more dignified than ever.

Most important of all, dear Bob was far richer than his father had been and even his older brother. His riches were evident around town—from the expensive apartments he rented out in the village to the rolling green acres of farmland in the surrounding hamlets. Men proudly greeted him in the streets. Women flaunted jewels manufactured by Ruckstein & Sons. Boys and girls flocked to the seasonal festivals put on in the big village hall in his honor. It seemed there was nothing that his hands had not touched in their little county that had not contributed to some good for all the people.

Madeline dreamily lifted her left hand, admiring the fancy ring on her finger, pleased that her husband loved her more than all—enough to give her the best out of all of his jewelry stores. Her eyes blinked back into reality as she saw the plain silver band and remembered, after all, that Ted Barker had been a poor man, as had been Sam Dunn before him.

Angrily stabbing the last envelope open, Madeline jabbed herself in the thumb and jolted in her seat as the prick of pain registered harshly in her brain. Putting aside the metal implement and letter together in dismay, she clutched her injured digit and rocked back and forth, bemoaning the fate that forced poverty upon her. She, past retirement age, was still forced to work and support herself. She, twice married and once widowed, had still been unable to find happiness and true love.

Seeing the hands of the clock slowly moving toward noon, Madeline rose with a sigh. So much for her attempt at sweet revenge. The world moved on and forced her to face reality. She pushed the prepared mail together in a heap. Her assistant would arrive shortly, and in the meantime, lunch would do her good.

Chapter Twelve

Saint George and the Dragon

I t was 5:48 on the evening of July 25 when Silvia Pearson burst through the door and tossed her keys on the kitchen counter with a loud groan.

Mom turned from the stove and looked at her daughter in surprise. "What's wrong?" she wondered, the wooden spoon in her hand dripping tomato sauce on the floor, narrowly missing her feet.

"Oh," Mom said, realizing what she was doing. She tittered at herself as she replaced the spoon in the sauce pot. "Dinner will be ready in ten minutes."

"I'm late. I can't eat right now." Silvia's words were sharply punctuated. She left the kitchen and went into her bedroom as quickly as she could. She changed her pants into capris and put on different shoes. She did not change her shirt and kept the same purse, but she reapplied her makeup as quickly as she knew how.

Silvia returned to the kitchen to grab her keys. "I'm going to VBS," she said to her mother's back.

Mom turned around, this time without the wooden spoon, and looked at her daughter with the same surprise as before. "VBS? Looking like that?" she said and began to laugh.

"Hey!" Silvia said angrily. "You never know!" She walked out the door with the same loud groan, got in her car, and quickly drove away.

Silvia arrived at church nearly half an hour after the first Vacation Bible School session had already begun. She struggled to maintain her composure as she walked in and found herself confronted by a sea of children seated on mats, all separated by age and engaged in a variety of activities. She felt awkward, not having an assigned task, and besides that, she was hungry.

Sneaking a chip from a nearby snack table, Silvia found a spot on a wooden bench against the wall and listened to the Bible lesson. Eventually, the lesson was over and some of the smallest children found her, so she spent the next fifteen minutes covered in excited children who were much too happy to share their constant giggles and misplaced saliva.

Promptly at seven o'clock, the tiny, squirming humans were called away to crafts, and Silvia began cleaning up the crunched goldfish and spilled juice left behind on the bench. She was wiping off a spot of slobber from her capris when a young man suddenly appeared and sat on the bench next to her.

"Good thing to get rid of that kiddy slime," he remarked. "It might seep in somewhere and contaminate your blood!"

Silvia glanced at the impertinent fellow and frowned slightly, but she did her best to ignore him as she continued to dab away at the wet spot. Finally satisfied with her efforts, she rose to toss away the tissues and paper towels. When she returned to the bench, the young man had his phone out.

"So, I've been to a lot of single retreats," he said out of the blue.

"Um, okay?" Silvia replied, baffled at such an announcement. "So have I."

"I don't suppose I've met you at any," he said dubiously, glancing at her quickly and then back at his phone.

"Definitely not," she murmured, her brow still wrinkled.

"Okay, then," he said, undeterred, as he continued to scroll through his contacts. "But tell me this, did I ever get your phone number?"

"Um, no," she said, even more bewildered, but she did not hesitate to give her number to him, looking admiringly at the state of his wardrobe and the charming manner in which he combed his hair.

"I'm George," the fellow finally introduced himself with a smile, putting his phone down and greeting her with a pair of clear blue eyes and a set of bright white teeth.

"George?" Silvia said skeptically, immediately regretting that she had conceded to grant him his wish concerning her digits. He was as good-looking as any fellow might hope to be, but she hated that name. Three and a half years ago, she had secretly promised herself never to marry a man named George.

"Well," he said a bit sheepishly, "that's my middle name, and it's what all my friends call me. But my real name is Brennan. That's what my family calls me, anyway."

"Brennan," she said, feeling suddenly relieved. "What an unusual name. What does it mean?"

"Actually," George, or Brennan, replied, "I don't really remember. My mom told me a couple of times, my whole name is kind of an old family thing, but I don't remember. Anyway, what's your name?"

"Silvia Pearson," she replied primly. "And my first name means that I am from the woods, which is not strictly true, since I live in the suburbs, and I hope to God that I never have to live in the middle of nowhere!"

Brennan laughed a bit but did not seem to mind. "Well, after we suffer through the rest of the week with child slime and cracker crumbs, we should go out sometime."

Silvia glanced up to see an army of children marching their way and quickly nodded, agreeable to that idea.

After going on a casual date that weekend, Brennan and Silvia were nearly inseparable, meeting at least twice a week and texting or talking almost daily.

"He's a great guy," Silvia told her mom after returning from one of their evening excursions. "He treats me decently like a man should, he has a lot of money, he's neat and clean, and his manners are impeccable."

"Outward appearances and material wealth aren't everything," her mom said pointedly, peering over the edge of her book. Her mother was a religious person, always taking great interest in all things related to God. "The important thing is that this young man you are infatuated with is a godly and righteous person."

"Yes, he is," Silvia said, rolling her eyes. "I was just getting to that. He goes to church every Sunday and Wednesday, he is a hard worker, he doesn't swear or drink, he believes in providing for his family, and," she concluded dramatically, "he agrees with me on the matters of women not having to work outside the home and education through homeschooling."

Mom said nothing further but simply gazed at her daughter.

"He has his own car, and he has a truck, and he has his own house!" Silvia said, now becoming angry. "I'm going to go visit his place on Friday night. I'll let you know whether he lives like a slob or not, and then you can get off your high judgmental attitude and actually appreciate the fact that marriage is finally an option for me!"

"High judgmental attitude?" Mom said in surprise. "Silvia, my dear daughter, I have nothing whatsoever against Brennan, or George, or whatever his name is."

"It's Brennan George MacDuff!" Silvia shot back, her face pink with irritation.

Mom laughed. "What a unique name, sounds very Scottish or Irish. I'm sure he is a great guy. You know, my grandmother used to talk a lot about a friend she had who was Gaelic. They can be very generous people, you know, but very angry and resentful when provoked."

Shaking her head a bit, Mom looked more seriously at her daughter. "My point, Silvia, is not to criticize Brennan, or any of the other guys you want to date. But think about what is most important—not so much if the guy meets all of your standards, but if he meets the Lord's!"

"Well, the Lord gave me my standards, so I expect a potential husband to meet them as well," Silvia said sharply and marched from the room. Her mother's words bothered her for a while, and then she finally texted her thoughts to Brennan.

"It makes me indignant," she wrote. "Some people judge and criticize the way that others look at the world, but they are basically doing the same thing to them!"

"Yes, what a conundrum," Brennan texted back twenty minutes later. "I'll call in an hour, and we can talk about it if you want. I'm finishing up a project."

"I'm going to bed," Silvia replied shortly, and shut off her phone for the night. He irritated her, too, sometimes, but she felt like all of his good qualities masked his flaws.

The real test came on Friday night. Silvia showed up at Brennan's place at 5:53 for their 6 PM dinner. Brennan had said he was going to cook for her, which amazed and intrigued her, and she hoped and prayed that the meal would turn out well.

His house appeared a bit rustic. It was an older Cape Cod with a barn and several sheds in the back, and the property was relatively remote according to Silvia's standards. She did not let those thoughts bother her too much, since she was well aware of the fact that he had enough money and enough brains to improve the current situation or move to another place, should that need arise.

Seeing both his car and his truck in the driveway, Silvia confidently parked, checked her makeup, and went up to the front door to ring the doorbell. Not finding one, however, she opted to rap several times on the window pane and then was about to return to her car for her phone to call him when he opened the door.

"Hello," he said, appearing a bit more subdued than normal. "Please come in."

Silvia went in, immediately smelling something delicious and was about to comment on it when she spotted a terrarium in the other room.

"What's that?" she asked, suddenly curious.

"Well," Brennan began slowly, sounding a bit nervous, "those are my family pets."

Silvia went forward a couple of steps, her high-heeled shoes making little thuds on the wide-board wooden floor. As she reached the doorway between the kitchen and the living room, she realized that there was not one but two large terrariums, each of them across the room from the other. One held a large brown python, and the other had a large green python.

Silvia froze momentarily and then forgot all of her manners, rushing across the room to get a better look. Yes, indeed, the second was a green tree python. She had seen one at a distance as a child and had always dreamed about owning one for a good part of her adolescence, but she had never had the good fortune to be this close to one.

Brennan's voice held an edge of nervousness as he walked up beside her and quietly explained, "This is Sally. I've had her for about five years, so she's still pretty young. Drag, this old guy over here, is probably going on twenty-something. I got him from my great-aunt."

Silvia turned and looked at Brennan in amazement. "You've had snakes this whole time and didn't bother to tell me about it? And, more than that, you've had *pythons* and didn't say a word about them?"

"Snakes are not a popular pet," Brennan replied quietly. "And most women don't want anything to do with them."

"True," she acknowledged, turning back to gaze at Sally, the green tree python. "Is she friendly?"

"She is, yes," Brennan said. "Drag is a bit of an ornery old fellow, but I take Sally out quite a bit. Here," he offered, going up to unlatch the lid. He put his hand in, causing Sally to flick out her tongue once or twice before obligingly reaching out and climbing up his wrist, his arm, and then settling herself casually across his shoulders as if to greet him like an old friend.

Brennan stood there with Sally looped across his shoulders and arms, but his eyes were on Silvia the whole time.

As for Silvia, when she got over the amazement of the fact that her nearly official boyfriend was the casual owner of not one but two pythons, she was not sure whether to be angry and slap him or to reach up and kiss him. Since he was still holding Sally, however, she opted for an entirely different route, asking if she could give it a try herself.

"Sure," Brennan said, turning slightly so that Sally's head faced Silvia's direction. "Hold up your elbow so she knows you are big enough to support her. He spent a moment trying to coax Sally to climb down from him to Silvia, but though the python flicked her tongue out a couple times to figure out the newcomer, she rebuffed all his attempts to move her. Sally was perfectly content hanging out on her owner's broad shoulders.

"Oh well, it takes some time," Brennan said in an apologetic tone, allowing Sally to slither back into her terrarium and carefully latching the lid again. "I need to check the chicken. It should be done now."

Silvia and Brennan spent a pleasant evening together, eating a delicious meal and talking for a while in the living room until it grew dark and Silvia became tired. As she drove home that night, she felt that something had changed in their relationship, but she could not put her finger on it.

Two weeks later, however, after she happily agreed to Brennan's request that she officially become his girlfriend, Silvia figured out what had changed between them.

"Sally is jealous of me," she told her mom, leaning over the porch railing as she looked down at the flowerbeds.

Mom looked up at her in surprise, her hands diligently pulling up weeds and her cheeks smudged with dirt from constantly brushing hair out of her face. "The snake? Jealous of you?"

"Yeah, that's what I think," Silvia said. "I don't think Brennan can tell, though."

"Why don't you tell him?"

"I have a better plan," Silvia said, smirking to herself. She went inside and glanced at the clock. She was supposed to meet Brennan at his house at 5:45, since that was when he got home from work, and then they were going out to meet his parents. She decided to leave a bit early and settle things on her own.

Silvia arrived at Brennan's place at 5:32 and glanced around the property carefully before getting out of the car. His truck was missing, so she decided she was safe.

Going up to the side door, she tried the handle and found it unlocked, just like she thought it would be. That was the one thing that bothered her—his front door had a lock, but the side door did not.

"I'll fix it sometime," Brennan told her last week when she brought it up. "Right now, it's not that big of a deal, anyway. No one comes up this road except the neighbors, and everyone knows each other. What are people going to steal from me anyway?"

"You never know," Silvia said aloud in the same prim tone of voice that she had used when she had answered Brennan. Carefully stepping around a bunch of old tools and scrap metal that he had left in the side room, she went through the squeaky door into the hallway and then down past the downstairs bathroom and bedroom into the living room.

Both pythons were quietly resting on their perches. Drag made no movement at all as she walked by his terrarium, but Sally raised her head a bit and then turned away, as if she recognized Silvia and could not be bothered with her presence.

Boldly, Silvia went up to Sally's pen, unhooked the lid, and reached inside. Sally's tongue flickered a couple of times, but then she hid her head under one of the loops of her body and became still.

"You want to avoid me, don't you?" Silvia said pointedly, touching the snake's smooth skin gently. "Well, guess what. You can't." Reaching in further, she moved her hand slowly up the python's neck until she found the spot right where the neck and head connected. Suddenly wrapping her fingers around Sally's throat, Silvia dragged the snake halfway out of the terrarium without warning, pulling her head up to stare straight into her mysterious yellow eyes.

"Guess what, Sally," Silvia said in a chilly voice. "You can be jealous all you want, but he is mine, Brennan is, and you're not going to get between us. So you can forget about it. If you want to be friendly with me, that would be great.

I have no hard feelings toward you. In fact, you're rather pretty. But I am the boss, and don't you forget it."

Shoving the python back into her pen, Silvia closed the lid a bit roughly and locked it. She glared at Sally, who was eagerly curling herself back into a mass of tight loops and hiding her head again, and then turned away with a satisfied air.

Then Silvia noticed that Drag was uncharacteristically moving around his pen, extending his long neck up to the top of the cage and pushing against the lid, and then traveling around the whole length of the terrarium before repeating the movement again. She went over to him and stared inside.

"And what do you have to say for yourself?" she said in a snippy voice. Hearing the sound of a truck outside, she turned and quickly went to the window. It was the UPS dropping off a large box on the porch.

Her mission accomplished, Silvia went into the kitchen and left through the front door, carefully locking it behind her. She glanced at her watch and realized that it was 5:43. Feeling satisfied again, she glanced at the newly arrived box with some curiosity and then sat down in the old rocker to wait for Brennan.

He arrived five minutes later and was apologetic for being late, but Silvia felt like being in a particularly gracious mood.

"No worries," she said happily, waving his apologies aside. "Go get changed while I wait here. It's a beautiful day, anyway."

"Yes, it is," Brennan said, looking at her a bit curiously. Then he smiled and unlocked the door. "Come on in and wait in the living room. It's more comfortable than that old chair."

Silvia got up willingly and followed him into the living room, glancing at each of the pythons in turn, but both of them were quietly resting as usual.

"Hey guys," Brennan said casually, checking their water dishes and then opening up Sally's lid to let her out for a bit. "What's going on, girl?" he wondered, stroking her head as she climbed up to rest on his shoulders. "Feeling sleepy today?"

Silvia came up to him and said, "Let me take her for a bit while you get changed."

"Okay," he said dubiously, knowing that their previous attempts to share the python had not been very successful.

But Sally willingly went to Silvia and made herself comfortable on her shoulders.

"Well, look at that," Brennan said happily, "I guess she finally warmed up to you!" He reached out to Sally, but she turned her head away and clung tighter to Silvia.

Brennan seemed even more surprised. "Well, I guess she has a new favorite!"

"Now, don't you start getting jealous," Silvia said teasingly.

At that, Brennan just laughed. "Over a snake?" He turned to leave. "If you get tired of her, just put her back in her pen. I'll be back in a jiffy."

After that successful turn of events, Silvia felt quite pleased and happy with her life. She had a delightful evening meeting Brennan's parents and married sister and brother-in-law, who were all very affable people, and felt very satisfied as they drove back to his house.

"Are you okay driving back home this late, or do you want me to drop you off?" Brennan asked as they pulled into the driveway at 10:03 PM.

Silvia smiled, feeling touched at his kindness and consideration. "I'll be fine," she promised.

The summer turned into fall, the fall marched steadily toward winter, and Silvia found herself meeting the rest of Brennan's family around Thanksgiving, so she introduced him to her family near Christmas. Then the winter turned colder, but on Valentine's Day, Silvia felt especially warm when Brennan gave her a ring. It was a beautiful little thing with designs of a snake's head carved in an emerald setting with little ruby eyes.

"It's a promise ring," he explained as he offered it to her, briefly mentioning its historic family value. Then he dropped the hint that he was saving up for a more important ring, one that he hoped to give her in the summer. "And after that, well—" and he left the rest of the phrase dangling and smiled at her as he had never smiled before.

As for Silvia, she was as happy as she had ever been, and she wore the ring proudly, though still on her right hand since they were not officially engaged.

"Sometimes I wonder," she told her mother one night, "Will it all work out? In some ways, Brennan seems too good to be true. You know what I mean? Like I feel that I might wake up one day and he'll be gone." She laughed at her own words, disbelieving herself, but as if to prove her point, she held her arm out to her mother. "Pinch me!"

Mom sat on a tall stool by the kitchen counter, jotting down a couple of to-do notes. She put down her pen and looked at her daughter thoughtfully but did not laugh along with her or make a move to pinch her daughter's arm.

"You aren't happy for me, Mom?" Silvia said in a hurt tone.

Mom's tone was kind but firm. "I'm afraid that you are putting too many hopes in Brennan, my dear. He is as fine a young man as any girl may ever hope to marry, yes, but no one deserves the kind of pressure that you are putting on him."

"Pressure! What kind of pressure am I putting on him?"

Mom sighed at that and turned to face her daughter directly. "Brennan is not perfect, Silvia. He is human, just like all of us. He makes mistakes, and he is going to disappoint you badly at some point if you expect him to be too good to be true."

"I know he's not perfect," Silvia argued. "He doesn't wash his car, he doesn't put a lock on his side door, he leaves his dishes in the sink for days at a time, he forgets to brush his teeth sometimes, and oh, a bunch of other things! But on all of the most important things, he is great, and we agree on everything."

"Everything?" Mom said skeptically.

Silvia shrugged. "Pretty much everything that I can think of." Before Mom could say anything else, Silvia burst out nastily, "You're just trying to make me morbid and think about all the bad things that can happen because of what happened to you!" She felt a bit of a pang as she saw the sadness suddenly cross her mother's face, for they both knew Silvia was bringing up the awful reminder of how her father had tragically died in a car accident ten years ago.

But Silvia wasn't done. "I miss Dad every day, and you just act like it was all part of God's will!"

"I miss him every day, too, Silvia," Mom said quietly, quickly recovering from her surprise. "I miss him more than you know. But I always knew that he would die before me, so I had to be prepared for that. I just didn't know when God would take him, but God provided the grace for that as well."

"Oh, you just don't understand!" Silvia said angrily, storming from the room. She closed and locked her bedroom door and then sat down to pray until she felt properly justified for being so angry about the situation.

Some time later, Silvia rose and looked at the little plaque above her desk. "Everyone deserves a happily ever after," it read, something that a friend from back in college had given her after Silvia had been a bridesmaid in her wedding. The friend had since had two children, gotten divorced, and moved back in with her parents, but as far as Silvia knew, Emily did not regret any of her choices for a moment. Even if happily ever after only lasted for a very short while, it was better than nothing.

Silvia shrugged, looked through her closet for her next day's workwear, and decided to call Brennan before retiring for the night.

Then winter turned into spring, and one rainy day in late spring found Silvia driving up the familiar road to Brennan's house. He had faced a very busy weekend, and she wanted to check in with him in person, even though they were planning to see each other on Wednesday as they usually did.

The thunder started just as she stepped out of the car, even though the rain had momentarily ceased, which she was very glad of, so it did not spoil her hair or clothes. Silvia went up to the front door and knocked, but there was no answer except a flash of lightning and another loud crack of thunder.

"Brennan?" she called at the open window, thinking about going to the unlocked side door, but she really did not feel like navigating through the junk room in the dark. She was just about to leave the porch when she heard a strange sound inside and turned to see a large black and brown dog standing by the window, staring at her.

Silvia started a bit and stared back at the dog, until another flash of lightning and peal of thunder put her back in motion. As she retreated hastily back to her car, she wondered where the dog had come from. Brennan did not have any other pets besides the two pythons and, as far as she knew, he did not have plans to obtain any more animals.

She got back into her car and called him, but there was no answer. Ending the call just as the voicemail message began, she drove up past the house to the barn, thinking that he might be in there. Both his truck and car were in the driveway, so Silvia got out quickly and went up to the barn door, knocking before trying to open it up.

It was locked from the inside, and just at that moment, she heard a terrific barking and scrabbling on the other side of the door. Then the wind picked up and the thunder and lightning started up again, all threatening to bring the torrential downpour that was imminent.

Crossly, and feeling a bit worried, Silvia returned to her car and wondered about all of the strange dogs as she carefully backed up and headed home in the driving rain. From the safety and comfort of her own home, she texted Brennan to see where he was and eagerly waited for a reply, but one did not come until the following morning.

"Sorry, had a busy day and a rough night," he replied. "How you doing?"

"Fine, the storm was terrible, but so glad it's over," Silvia replied during a lull in her work day. "Where did you get the dogs???"

"Watching them for some friends," came back the answer later on. "I'll explain later."

Despite his casual response, Silvia worried about it all day. Even after she talked to Brennan that afternoon and heard his thorough explanation about how his friends had convinced him to keep their two Rottweilers for a couple of days while they went on vacation, she was still unsettled.

That night, Silvia dreamed she was stuck in a thunderstorm in the middle of the night and could not find her way back home. When she finally caught a glimpse of light, she stumbled up to Brennan's house, made her way through the junk room, and found that the brown python was morphing into the same terrible black dog that she had seen through the window.

In the dream, Silvia screamed and ran out of the house before Drag could catch her, but then, when she sprinted toward the barn to hide from the monster, Brennan emerged from the doorway and began to shapeshift into a large black dog as well.

Silvia awoke with a start and sat straight up in bed. She looked at the clock. Its green glowing figures showed her that it was only 3:58 AM. She still had another two hours to sleep.

Silvia lay down again with relief, but the more she thought about it, she was filled with a great sense of dread. By the time the sun rose and Silvia got up for the day, she was convinced. Her happily ever after was coming to a swift end.

"What's the matter?" Mom asked over breakfast, instinctively knowing that something was wrong.

"Didn't you say that you knew someone Scottish or Irish from college?"

"My grandmother was best friends with a Gaelic girl for most of her life," Mom corrected. "I do not remember ever meeting her, but she would tell a lot of stories. Some of them were interesting, but most of them were fanciful. Why?"

"Oh, Brennan invited me over to a family picnic for July 4, and he said his great-aunt was coming from Ireland. She's really old, in her 90s, I think. I guess she used to live here, and then moved back to be with her daughter, and is coming to visit once more before she gets too old to travel. I just wondered if she was the person your grandmother talked about."

Mom was intrigued. "She very well may be! That would be fascinating if she were the same person! Wouldn't Grandma Gable love to see her again if she were still with us! I know she used to pray for her all the time. They were best friends, but Grandma doubted that she was saved, said she was more into mysticism than faith and trust in God."

"Oh well," Silvia said. "You're invited to the picnic, too, if you want to come. Guess I forgot to tell you when Brennan invited me."

"Thank you!" Mom said genuinely. "But I already made plans with Drew and Kathy and the kids," referring to Silvia's older brother and his wife and family. "They were asking about you, by the way. They said that they never see you anymore."

"Yeah, we all grow up and get busy," Silvia said dismissively, rising from the table and bringing her bowl to the sink. "Well, I'll see you later," she said, glancing at the clock and heading back to the bathroom to primp before going to work."

"See you," Mom said, watching her daughter's back thoughtfully as she disappeared around the corner.

July 4 was a beautiful day. Silvia went over to Brennan's house mid-morning to help him load up his truck with ice coolers and tables from church, and then they drove up to his parents' place where the afternoon picnic would be held.

On the drive up, Silvia thought about telling him about her dream, her mom's grandmother, and a thousand other trivial things, but she said nothing.

"What's eating you up, Sil?" Brennan asked at one point, glancing at her with a shining smile. His hair was perfectly gelled, and he was wearing a new shirt that matched his eyes.

Silvia felt a flash of pride, but then the feeling dissipated. "Nothing," she said lightly. "I was just thinking about some things I need to do." After a brief pause, she added, "I was thinking about the pythons, too, actually. You said that you got Drag from your great-aunt. Is that the same aunt who is going to be at the party today?"

"Oh, yeah," he said with a brief laugh. "I meant to warn you ahead of time. Don't mind Aunt Kelli, she's a little crazy, but she's a good lady. She's very old, and she's seen a lot, and she has an opinion about everything, but she wouldn't hurt a fly."

"Warn me?" Silvia wondered. "If she's so harmless, then what are you warning me about?"

"Oh, she's very nosy and pries into everyone's lives, that's all." Brennan laughed and began to tell a story about how Aunt Kelli used to write to him for years, demanding to know when he was going to marry so that she could send him some instructions about how to properly care for a wife.

"Sounds like a control freak!" Silvia said at last when his tale was over.

"Yeah, maybe in some ways, but she's a good lady and loves her family," Brennan concluded, smiling at Silvia and reaching over to take her hand.

It was a lovely day for a picnic, even with a touch of mugginess, and Silvia decided to try and enjoy herself. She found the food delicious, Brennan's family very welcoming, and Brennan himself the sweetest and most romantic that she had ever remembered him being. She began to wonder if he had other plans for that day besides the picnic, particularly involving a certain type of jewelry.

All of those ideas, however, were put aside shortly after three o'clock when a sudden thunderstorm rolled in, forcing everyone to quickly move inside for shelter. In the hubbub, Silvia found herself sitting in the living room across from the notorious Aunt Kelli, who had been talking to everyone in the whole family the whole morning and afternoon.

"Ah, Silvia, is it?" the old lady cackled, looking at Silvia from across her silver-rimmed glasses.

"Yes," Silvia replied, suddenly feeling a bit of dread steal over her. She glanced around for Brennan, but he was still outside, helping bring in all the tables before the downpour started.

"You look mighty familiar, girl. What's your last name?" Aunt Kelli prodded.

"Pearson," Silvia replied quietly.

"Hmm," the old lady said, shaking her head. "What is your mother's maiden name?"

"Crestwood," Silvia said in the same calm and straightforward tone as before.

Again, the shake of the head. "Your grandmother's maiden name?"

Silvia felt puzzled for a moment, as her grandmother had been married twice, but then she remembered. "Gilbert."

"Gilbert," Aunt Kelli said thoughtfully, tasting the word carefully. "Gilbert. It rings a bell, but no. Who was your grandmother's mother?"

"I never met her," Silvia said awkwardly, thinking back to the few conversations she remembered having with

Mom about her beloved Grandma Gable. After a moment, she added, "Mom always called her Grandma Gable, but I don't remember her full name."

"Gable!" the old woman cackled with delight. "Marjorie Gable! How well I remember that name! And the face!" She pointed straight at Silvia and cackled. "You have her eyes, and her chin, I believe, if I'm not mistaken, which I usually am not. She was Marjorie Dorland back in the day, but her married name was Gable, and that is the name I most commonly associate with her."

Silvia listened in a bit of wonder as the old woman rattled on and on about her great-grandmother's side of the family as if they were old friends, which they had been. Then she began to feel terribly awkward as Silvia realized that many of Brennan's relatives were crowding around to listen.

Seeing the audience around her growing, Aunt Kelli began to grow expansive. Pointing a bony finger at Silvia, she cackled for a moment and then said, "Set still, girl, and let me tell you a thing or two about your great-great-grandmother. This will be Marjorie's mother. Mrs. Dorland we called her, but she was a downright witch, that woman!

And I don't mean that in a good way, not like my kind of witch, the other kind."

And so began a tale from Kelli O'Hennessey's childhood, where she and her beloved best friend Marjie played a prank on Marjie's mother. It involved a certain number of reptiles and amphibians in the kitchen, resulting in both of them being soundly paddled for taking the liberty of amusing themselves in such a manner. As Silvia listened, she began to feel a bit uneasy, and that sensation only served to grow over the course of the story, even as the thunder and lightning continued to rage outside.

"And there I stood, in the middle of the kitchen, my bloomers around my ankles and my little bottom bright red from the beating," Aunt Kelli eagerly concluded her tale. "So, I looked right up at Marjie's mother—Mrs. Dorland, that is—and I said to her, 'A curse be on you, old hag, and may your descendants turn into dogs and snakes!'" Aunt Kelli cackled loudly and shook her head, looking around to see others in the room chuckling as well.

Silvia smiled a bit and looked down, more out of politeness than from a sense of feeling amused. In reality, she felt shocked, appalled, and shaken to her core, wondering about the significance of that curse from long ago and how it affected both the MacDuffs and the Pearsons.

Before Silvia had a chance to sort out her thoughts, Aunt Kelli was struggling to get up, loudly declaring to everyone that it was time for her to spend a good while in the little girl's room. Then, Brennan appeared at her elbow, rather wet and disheveled from the rain and hurried activity. He looked apologetic and disappointed, but refrained from complaining until they were back in his truck and headed home.

"A perfect day ruined," he said a bit miserably, trying to slick back his once-perfect hair.

"Don't worry about it," Silvia said to him, wondering at the fact that she did not share his grave disappointment. "We can go out on Friday, anyway."

"Yes," he said, glancing at her and suddenly smiling, "yes, let's, just the two of us. I feel like it's been too busy today, there've been too many people around."

She smiled back, but she felt like she was smiling more to herself than to him.

Brennan was still talking. "I hope Aunt Kelli didn't annoy you too much. I warned you that she is kind of crazy."

"It's okay." She hesitated a moment and then asked, "When did she give you Drag?"

"Oh, before she left the area, she told me some big long story about him and the significance of the meaning of his name, and all sorts of stuff, but I don't remember most of it anymore."

"Significance of the meaning of his name?" Silvia repeated. "What does that mean?"

Brennan appeared a bit disgusted. "Drag has a pedigree. His official name is 'Dragon King of the Black Woods,' or some such nonsense, but it's all in Welsh, I think, so I just call him Drag."

"Dragon King?" Silvia said in surprise. "Doesn't your first name mean 'king' in Welsh?"

He shrugged a bit. "It might."

Silvia sat back, reflecting on this new tidbit as the same uneasy feeling from before returned and then continued to grow. "Do you think her curse meant anything, then?"

"Whose curse?" Brennan said in surprise, glancing at her. "What are you talking about?"

"Did you hear Aunt Kelli's story?" Silvia wondered.

"I came in at the end when she was announcing she needed a bathroom break," he said with a displeased grunt.

"Old people and their bodily fluids really should not be up for public discussion."

At that, Silvia's ordinary sense of self-satisfaction finally began to return to her. "I agree," she said after a moment, feeling reoriented and content. "I think your aunt is pretty crazy." She glanced at Brennan, sighed, and shook her head. "I'm sorry."

He grinned at her. "Don't be. I warned you of that in the first place, anyway."

Early Friday evening, Brennan and Silvia met at a very nice restaurant, both wearing very fine clothes and acting in their very finest manners. They both appeared very happy and self-assured.

At the end of the meal, Brennan looked at Silvia very meaningfully and began to say some well-planned words, but she smiled at him a bit teasingly and shook her head to stop him.

"I have something to say first, Brenny," she murmured, taking off the little snake ring on her right hand.

He looked surprised but fell silent.

"I love you," she said to him passionately, reaching across the table and pressing the little ring into his hand, "but I cannot marry you."

Brennan's surprise turned to shock. "What are you talking about?"

A tear slipped from Silvia's eyes, but she quickly wiped it away as her words came out in a rush. "It would never work between us, Brenny. We agree on all the important things, and we go so well together, and you are a great provider, and everything is perfect, but I just can't. Something is just not right, and I just can't do this to you, or to myself, or to your family, or my family. It just has to stop."

"This is about my aunt and the story she told you, isn't it?" he said, his face becoming stern to prevent himself from appearing as devastated as he felt.

"No, no, it's not," she said desperately. "I felt this way before your aunt told the crazy story about the curse and all of that, or any of my strange dreams about you shapeshifting or any of that nonsense—it is something else, something I feel deeply but don't know how to explain."

Brennan scowled slightly. "A curse and shapeshifting? What in the h—Silvia, what on earth are you talking about?"

"Forget it," she said sharply. "I said, that isn't the main issue, it's something else."

"Well, then, what is it?"

Silvia gave a great sigh and sat back in her chair, staring at Brennan for a moment. "I just can't. You're a great guy, but I just can't deal with the inconsistency. We get together a couple times a week, and we call and talk sometimes, but you never get back to me right away, you always show up late, you—"

"Stop," Brennan said, disgusted. "You don't want a husband."

"What?" she said in surprise.

"You want a lapdog you can control all the time," he said sharply. "I'm not a lapdog. I'm a human being. I try to be on time, but I'm not at your constant beck and call. Other things come up, you know. I try to get back to you as soon as I can, but I'm not tied to this—this device all the time," he said, shoving away her phone that lay on the table between them, knocking it to the carpeted floor.

"I love you, Silvia, but the more that I get to know you, I don't even think you want a real-life husband to take care of you and to raise a family with. I think you just want a lapdog. You want a lapdog that will come when you call it, and go away when you don't want it around, and will eat whatever you want it to eat, and will make lots of money so you can live in a plush environment, and will make love to you whenever you want it to, but only then. And you know what—I'm glad you mentioned this now instead of later."

Brennan rose from his chair slightly and motioned to the waiter for the check.

Silvia stared at him, the tears now dripping off her chin. "Is that what you think of me?" she said, horrified.

Brennan stared back at her, his face red with anger. "I wish it could have turned out differently," he said after a moment, letting his temper cool down a bit. "I had my doubts from the beginning, but I thought—well, honestly, Sil, I thought that it would get better in time."

"I thought you were going to propose to me tonight!" she said miserably, ignoring everything he said.

He looked surprised, his face reddening but from em-barrassment. "I was—I mean, I thought I was going to. I mean—well, I bought a ring last week. I was going to give it to you after the July 4th picnic, but then it rained. And then you got cold all of a sudden, and I thought—well, I didn't know what happened. Something happened, but

I don't know what it was." Brennan gazed at her, his expression suddenly tender but his eyes distant, as if he was looking through her into the future. "But I understand now."

"What do you understand?" she wondered, wiping the tears off her face again.

Brennan thanked the waiter and picked up the bill from the table. He opened up his other hand, revealing the little snake ring. "That you don't want a husband. I want a wife, but I don't think you want a husband."

He rose from the table and looked at her with his bright blue eyes, his handsome face still flushed. "I'm sorry, Sil, I'll see you around sometime." He tucked the ring in his pocket, pulled out his wallet, the. Turned to the cashier counter with the bill between thumb and forefinger.

Silvia sat rigidly at the table, her face stormy as she watched Brennan pay for the tab and head out into the fine summer evening in his perfectly tailored suit. She waited a moment and then got up, retrieving her phone from the floor before snatching up her purse and marching out to escape the curious stares of the other diners.

Once in her car, Silvia allowed herself time to think and cry and generally let out her hurt emotions. Then, at precisely 6:30 PM, she collected herself, started her vehicle, and drove home as if nothing had ever happened.

The following Monday, Silvia got home from work and stormed through the door at 5:31. Her mom was standing at the stove, as usual, and turned to greet her with a cheery hello.

"Hi, Mom," she said brusquely, and then went to look at the calendar where her mom had scribbled down the church events for the week.

"How was your day?" Mom asked, stirring dinner carefully.

"Fine," Silvia called back over her shoulder, quickly going up to her room. She changed her shirt, but not her skirt, and then she changed her shoes, but not her purse. She took off her necklace, put on some more makeup, and then went back downstairs.

"I'm going to VBS," she announced, grabbing her keys from the counter where she dropped them. "Don't wait up for me."

Mom turned in surprise, her wooden spoon dripping red sauce onto the floor. "VBS?" she marveled, and then her amazement grew as she noticed what Silvia was wearing. "Looking like that? What happened with George?"

"It's Brennan!" Silvia snapped. "He and I are no longer an item! He doesn't want me. He wants a bedraggled hick for a wife!"

As the door slammed behind her daughter, Mom stood there in wonder for a moment longer before turning back to the stove, her prayers rising like the steam coming off the chili.

CHAPTER THIRTEEN

On Matchmaking and Falling in Love

Michael Sirani was sitting at his desk in his bedroom and working on an online class assignment when a hasty knock interrupted his thoughts. Before he had a chance to answer, he raised his head to see the door crash open, his twin sister Mabel bursting in, all out of breath.

"Oh, Mikey, run! Fly! Flee!" she said dramatically, collapsing a few feet away on his neatly made bed.

Turning away from his books, Mike scowled at her. "What is it, May-May?" he demanded. "I do not have time for any shenanigans."

Composing herself, Mabel said with seriousness, "This is not a mere shenanigan, sir. Annabelle and her mother are here. I just saw them drive in."

Mike snorted and turned back to his desk. "No concern of mine! You go down there and make them some sweet tea."

"But you have to get out of here!" Mabel said desperately, rising and approaching her brother.

"And what exactly are you suggesting that I do, pray tell?" he asked sarcastically, not even bothering to look up as he turned a page in his textbook.

"Fake a fire call! Say you just have to go somewhere! Or, I know! This one is more realistic—say that Joe needs you at the store to fill in for Bobby!"

"Just go away and close the door," Mike said sourly. "I'm working on an assignment that I need to finish by 3."

"Oh!" Mabel was suddenly happy. "Perfect!" She went to the doorway and glanced back at her brother before closing the door. "Goodbye," she whispered and then merrily went downstairs, hearing her mom, Mrs. Murphy, and Annabelle chatting in the kitchen as the teapot began to whistle.

Drawing in a deep breath, Mabel walked calmly into the dining room to find them seated at the little round table by the bay window.

"Oh, Mabel, dear," Annabelle said sweetly in her perfect Carolinian accent, rising to give her newly met friend an embrace. "How are you?"

"Great, you?" Mabel said casually, slipping from the sticky hug to sit down in the nearest empty chair.

"Oh, wonderful," Annabelle replied, going on to talk about how beautiful the Michigan summertime was, how lovely and green the countryside looked, and all manner of all sorts of things.

Mabel sat there and politely listened, asking questions when appropriate while also keeping her other ear on her mom's inquiries about Murphy's General Store in Raleigh. She was the picture of an attentive host, but all that she could truly think about was how Annabelle Murphy came to be occupying a chair at the Sirani household in the first place. Yes, she was a nice girl and, yes, her family sounded decent, but she had no business waltzing into their lives to try and get to know Mabel's beloved twin brother.

Regardless of her innermost sentiments, Mabel endured the whole hour and a half of hospitable entertainment as politely as she knew how, not only talking to Annabelle over tea, but also taking her out to see their fruit trees, vegetable gardens, chickens, and ducks. After Mrs. Murphy and Annabelle had left, however, Mabel was quite ready to speak a good piece about how indignant she felt.

Fortunately, her mom beat her to it, and that was just as her dad arrived home from picking up a stack of lumber for an older neighbor's barn project, his two younger sons in tow.

"I really can't believe it!" Mom said, tossing herbs over a couple of chickens before placing the roaster in the oven for supper. Turning around to shush Jimmy and Patrick's squabbling about truck brands, she went on. "I really want to give Lily Adams a piece of my mind, that woman!"

Seeing that her husband's attention was fixed on her, the family matriarch went on. "Now don't get me wrong—Jill and Annabelle are perfectly nice people, but the whole drama Lily has created—ugh! It is disgusting!"

Mabel had heard enough. She knew that her dad was adequately interested and that her mom would carry on for some time, so she retreated from the kitchen to go upstairs to her room and gloat over the fact that she had successfully kept Annabelle from her brother that day. Not only that, but she had learned that the Murphy ladies would be going back home on Tuesday, so there was only Sunday to get through. Then that would be the end of that.

When she thought about the situation from the other girl's point of view, however, Mabel couldn't help but feel a little bad for Annabelle. Here was a young woman who looked exquisitely beautiful with her long blonde hair, gentle blue eyes, perfect pink lipstick, carefully pressed clothes, and impeccable Southern manners. Plus, Annabelle was probably completely unaware of how rude people from the north could be in comparison to her type of folk.

Mabel imagined that Annabelle had felt sad at the way Mike gave her a brusque greeting on Friday night when they were all introduced at their church's college and career group. The sweet southern belle had probably been looking forward to getting to know him, based on how the nosy Lily Adams had portrayed him. As devoted as she was to her twin, Mabel knew full well that he was no proper, elegant fellow with the gentlemanly manners that Annabelle was accustomed to.

Later that evening, as Mike and Mabel sat in the living room after their parents and younger siblings had gone to bed, Mabel decided to ask her brother what he thought. Putting down her book, she looked at Mike as he was comfortably slouched across the nearby couch, playing a video game on the TV.

She asked him, "Do you feel bad for Annabelle?"

He glanced over at her with a bit of surprise and then said shortly, "'Course not. Why should I?"

"Oh, you know, the whole thing is ridiculous, but what if she's just going along with Mrs. Adams's plans, her parents wanting her to get married, and all that?"

"She didn't *have* to come up here to try to meet me," he said pointedly. "That's what social media is for, anyway. Wasting the time to come up is like low-key stalking, Christian style."

May tittered slightly. "Maybe, but still. What do you think of her?"

Mike shrugged. "Nothing. You talked to her, May-May. What did *you* think?"

"She's too desperate to get married," May replied honestly with a grimace. "If it wasn't for that, I think she would be nice. But she hardly does anything, and her hands are too soft."

"Well, then, there you go, not my kind of girl," Mike said with a yawn, settling down again. After a moment, he glanced at his sister. "Is she gonna be at church tomorrow?"

"Yes, but then they're leaving Tuesday."

"Good," he said gruffly and then went back to his game.

May picked up her book again, but she couldn't help worrying a bit that the drama was far from over.

Much to Mabel's relief, however, the following day was very average. The only part that made her squirm was a brief farewell scenario led by the dramatic Mrs. Lily Adams that included Mrs. Murphy, Annabelle, her mom, and her younger sister. But Mike was spared any hassle, fortunately, and he only smirked slightly when his dad inquired over lunch if he had the chance to say goodbye to the southern belle.

The incident soon passed from regular family conversation and only came up whenever their mom cleaned house for Mrs. Adams on Tuesdays.

"Apparently," Mom said to her husband at supper one evening, "Lily is greatly regretting her failed experiment with Mike. I asked her if that meant she would give up her gossiping and meddling in everybody's lives, but oh no! That woman is ridiculous!"

"Now what?" Jimmy piped in, greatly intrigued by all the goings on.

Lifting her eyes to Mabel at the end of the table, Mom continued by waving her fork in her eldest daughter's direction. "And you just watch out! Because you are next!"

"Me?" squawked Mabel in shock while Mike choked on his salad and the rest of the table erupted in laughter. It was a well-known fact in the household that Mabel was adamantly opposed to romance for herself of any sort, though no one was quite sure whether it was a defense against nonsense in general or because she actually did not like the thought of marriage.

But after that, Mabel did keep her eyes and ears open, soon discovering that her mom was correct. Lily Adams had set her sights on a young fellow named Richard P.

Brighton as a potential match for Mabel. This prospect was moving to the area at the insistence of his grandparents who were long-time locals. He had just completed his master's at a prestigious university and accepted a position at a well-paying job with great benefits. Plus, he had purchased a nice car and started renting an apartment while doing some house-shopping, so he generally had everything going for him. Except that he needed a wife.

"He's popular and outgoing," Mike teased his sister after they returned from an evening church service. Richard had not been there, but there had been plenty of talk about him.

"Riveting," she said dully, closing the door behind them and locking them in for the night.

"He's handsome and brilliant!" Mike added, the enthusiasm fading from his voice.

His sister pointedly ignored him.

At that, Mike shook his head. "People should just mind their own business and leave us out of it."

"Amen," May said fervently.

The following month, a special Sunday afternoon conference was held that the Sirani family attended. When they drove in for morning worship, the matchmaking situation was the furthest thing from any of their minds, but when Mom spotted a group of church gossips fawning around a certain well-groomed young fellow, she groaned and made a snide comment under her breath. She turned to look at her eldest daughter, but Mabel had already left the van and was walking steadily and undistractedly toward the church's front doors with June at her right hand and Patrick on her left.

Mabel had seen Richard all right, dressed up in his neat suit and his shiny shoes, and she did her best to avoid running into him all day. Not only that, but she also steered clear of Pastor John, the pastor's wife, Lily Adams, and anyone else who looked too long in her direction. It was not that Richard was ugly or weird, but the awkwardness of the situation was enough for her to permanently avoid him.

After lunch and the conference lecture, Mike, Mabel, and a group of other young people gathered in one of the Sunday school rooms before the start of the last breakout session, when who should walk in but Richard P. Brighton.

Mabel was sitting in a wooden chair against one wall, watching several small children playing on the floor while chatting with Nancy, her friend and one of the young mothers in the congregation. Mabel glanced up to find the fellow's eyes upon her, and Nancy immediately fell silent. Not feeling particularly friendly, Mabel simply sat there, and the two of them sized each other up for a moment or two.

Then Richard rocked back on his heels slightly, smiled a bit, and then said casually, "So, the famous Miss Mabel Sirani, I presume." Without awaiting any reply, the bold fellow presumptuously went on, "Let me ask you, Miss Sirani, what are your inclinations toward courtship?"

Mabel felt her face flush as the room went deathly silent and everyone's gaze settled on her. The only remaining noises in the room were from the three little kids on the floor who continued playing with blocks and trucks without a care in the world. Mabel wished the chair would suddenly crush her in its grasp, demolishing her along with the mortification she felt at that particular moment.

But Richard was still watching, and he still expected an answer.

Mabel began timidly, "Well, I have not particularly considered courtship for myself." Feeling that her honest reply was unsatisfactory, she went on, "Though, I suppose it is as fine an institution as any, for those who are inclined to it, and it would be fine for me or any other single person to get married if the Lord so called—but being single is just as good," she ended in a rush, feeling a sense of distaste and hypocrisy rising in her throat.

Richard smiled affably at that juncture. "Point granted, but I mean to ask how the situation applies to you particularly, since I would like to continue pursuing unless you say otherwise."

Mabel had absolutely no words for such an impertinent statement, but fortunately for her, Mr. Jones, the elder in charge of their breakout session, came in at that precise moment. He was a no-nonsense farmer and possessed a great booming voice, so he wasted no time in calling the group to order, adding the admonition that they were already a few minutes behind schedule because he had been required to herd in a couple of stragglers.

So, with that, Richard promptly smiled at Mabel and sat down in the chair directly across from her. As for Mabel, she remained quietly seated in her chair for the whole session, hardly moving a muscle, not even to look at Mike once. The only time she moved significantly was halfway through the session when she leaned down to retrieve a toy for one fussy child who had tossed it quite out of reach.

Otherwise, poor Mabel was so distracted by the odd situation that she hardly heard a word from Mr. Jones or any of the comments that others offered, not even any of the intelligent sentiments that Richard contributed. She just sat there and stared at the open Bible in her lap, occasionally jotting down a few words in her notepad. But even that activity did not focus or calm her buzzing mind.

In fact, as the hour slowly came to an end, Mabel began to feel ill to the point of doing the unthinkable—getting up in the middle of the closing prayer and hiding out in the ladies' room for a full twenty minutes.

At 3:50, June came looking for her older sister, finding Mabel standing by the sink farthest from the door, washing her hands.

"Are you okay?" June asked, peering up into her big sister's face.

Mabel smiled slightly. "Yes," she said calmly. "How did you like the conference?"

June sighed. "It was fine, but too long. I forgot everything about it already."

"Me, too," Mabel admitted.

"We're going home now," June offered after a pause.

"Good." Mabel dried her hands, picked up her Bible and notepad from the nearby shelf, and steadily led the way—out of the bathroom, out to the foyer, through the double doors, past the lingering groups of chatty people, across the parking lot, and into the family vehicle without hesitation or delay.

She saw her dad give her a brief searching look, and her mom whipped around in her seat to ask what happened. Mabel merely gave both parents a tiny smile and asked, "Did Mike leave already?" When her dad replied in the affirmative, Mabel kept her chin up and her eyes straight ahead, remaining completely silent for the whole fifteen-minute drive home.

Later after supper, however, once the family stopped pestering her about why she was so quiet, Mabel cornered her twin brother in the mudroom. Mike was looking over his climbing equipment for the next workday.

"What's up, May-May?" he said a bit gruffly from his position on a nearby crate as he checked his boots over.

"What's up?" she nearly screeched, though keeping her voice level and at a volume hardly above a whisper. "Richard P. Brighton is up, that's what! And while I'm certain that he's a fine fellow at heart, could he have been anymore weirder? I mean, come on!"

Imitating Richard's inflection of speaking, she quoted, "'What are your inclinations toward courtship?' Are you serious?! How about a simple, 'Hi, how are you today?' but oh, no! He has to jump right into the marriage topic, and I felt like my face was on fire, so what could I do in that situation but give some idiotic biblical-sounding answer and probably look like an absolute ninny!"

Mabel stopped to take a deep breath, attempting to calm down.

Mike looked up at his sister. "I thought your answer was fine," he said stolidly. "I mean, considering the bizarre situation presented to you."

"Well!" Mabel said, about to take off again, but then she checked herself and asked quietly, her tone exposing some grief, "Why didn't you step in? I was hoping for a little backup, or something—anything—but you didn't do anything. Why not?"

Mike looked up at her again, his face unreadable, but there was a strange glimmer in his eye that she did not recognize. "You mad at me, May-May?" he asked at length.

She swallowed hard. Finally, she admitted, "Kinda."

"Well, if it's any comfort to you, May," he said, going back to his polishing, "like I said before, you handled yourself just fine. What else could I have done to help you that would have been appropriate for the situation?"

Sighing loudly, she turned away and went to lean against the far wall. "Maybe just be there?" she suggested.

"I was there," he said, a bit hotly.

"I mean, maybe walk up and just stand nearby? Or maybe introduce yourself? I don't know. Were you even paying attention?"

"Everyone was," he growled.

She groaned again.

Mike dropped his boots in their spot and got up noisily to check his belt and ropes that were hanging on a hook on the wall. He didn't say anything for a bit, but then, finding everything in order, hung it back up neatly and turned toward his sister. Mabel was leaning against the wall next to the light switch, and his eyes met hers briefly.

"I was paying attention, May-May," he said quietly. "Don't be mad at me. Do you honestly think there was any way for me to do anything to help you without making a bigger mess of the situation?"

Mabel looked at him in surprise. "How could it have possibly been any worse?"

At that, a glimmer of a smile appeared on her twin's face, but then Mike leaned over and flicked off the light switch. "It's not recommended to roundhouse kick people in church, you know," he said dismissively, turning toward the lighted doorway that went into the kitchen.

Mabel suddenly felt herself flooded with warmth. Reaching out and grabbing Mike's sleeve before he could leave, she said, "Do you really mean that, Mike? Were you really that mad about it?"

"Of course I was mad, May-May," he said, brushing her off. But then he looked back at her as she followed him into the kitchen and smiled slightly, knowing her penchant for flowery adjectives. "In fact, I was utterly furious."

"Oh, thank you," she said, impulsively reaching out and hugging him tightly. "I thought no one cared. That was dumb. I'm sorry. I'm really sorry."

"It's okay, May-May," Mike said quietly, patting her on the back before she let go of him. "Anyway, I'm always here for you, you know."

The rest of the evening was very pleasant. Mabel was soon able to put Richard P. Brighton completely out of her mind, and the weeks that progressed into fall were full of happiness and peace.

Then, one September morning, Mabel woke up with the memory of an odd dream in which she and Mike both fell in love and got married. She felt rather vexed about that possibility for the whole day, even as she went about her work and school.

After nothing happened for several days, she resolved that if anything romantic was to happen to either of them, then it would have to happen to both of them. Content in her mind that nothing would happen for quite some years, Mabel happily forgot about her dream.

The last Saturday of that same month, Mabel woke up early and went downstairs to make breakfast before the family got up. She assumed that Mike had already gone out, since he had been preparing for hunting season that whole week by running every morning—and she confirmed her theory when she saw his water bottle waiting for his return by the sink. She felt happy and at peace with the world and soon had her hands covered in flour.

Just as she was pulling out a baking dish to grease for coffeecake, Mabel heard the sound of a truck pulling into the driveway. It did not sound like Mike's truck, and a horrible thought immediately occurred to her. She reluctantly turned at the sounds of a knock on the door, fully prepared to see the affable smile of Richard P. Brighton shining through the window.

Instead, there was a handsome and rugged-looking fellow with bright blue eyes standing there, waiting patiently with a couple of boxes of shotgun shells in hand.

Mabel suddenly felt a wave of shyness come over her as she pulled the door open and let him in.

"Hello," he said politely in a deep, friendly tone, and she acknowledged the greeting with a quiet response. For a few moments, they said nothing, but then he was introducing himself as Scott and Mabel was inviting him to sit down for a cup of coffee. Scott preferred to stand, but he was glad to take some coffee, so she gave him a mug and told him to help himself as she turned back to put the coffee cake batter in the pans. All the whole, she began to worry about why he was there and what he was doing.

Just then, Mike burst in, all out of breath and sweating from his run. "Hey, May-May," he said, and then, "Oh, hey, Scott, you're early. Great, you got the shells."

He grabbed his water bottle, chugged half of it, and then set it back down on the counter, turning to pick up the nearby boxes of shells. "I'm gonna hit the shower and get changed, be back in 5–and with your money," he said and then promptly disappeared around the corner toward the stairs.

Mabel took a deep breath and inadvertently let it out a bit loudly as she closed the oven door on the coffeecake.

Scott turned from the sink, having just finished stirring some cream into his coffee. "Did you burn yourself?" he asked with a bit of concern and then stepped toward her when she did not reply.

"No," she said, but her tone sounded more desperate than she intended.

"Then what's the matter?" he wondered, watching her steadily as she began to gather up the dirty dishes.

Mabel turned toward him, as he stood between her and the sink, and then let out everything in a sudden rush. "I don't know. Why are you here? I mean, besides waiting to go shooting with Mike. What do you want? Why get here early and come in instead of waiting outside?" Realizing how rude that sounded, she checked herself. "I don't mean to be rude. I just—I don't understand why you're looking at me all weirdly like that."

Scott looked at her desperation calmly with steady compassion and merely gave her a slight smile. Then he lowered his mug, swallowed slowly, and quietly replied, "Mike has told me a fair amount about his family and his siblings over the years that I've known him. He said his favorite sister Mabey was a little feisty, so maybe I was curious to meet you. You have a problem with that?"

"Maybe, but maybe not," Mabel said, her face flushing as her feeling of agitation grew. "I have no problem meeting anyone or being friends with guys, but the whole dating and matchmaking and courting and all the drama is repulsive to me, and I've had enough of it! So, if you're expecting some romantic situation or have some other ridiculous notion, you can give it up!"

Hearing Mike tromping down the stairs, she quickly walked past Scott to the sink and began running the water to wash the dishes.

"And that's that!" May said conclusively, picking up the dish detergent with a flourish and immediately calming herself down, though with somewhat of an effort.

"Ready to go?" Mike asked Scott, coming around the corner into the kitchen and pulling on his camo jacket. Then he noticed that Scott was watching his sister with a bemused smile on his face and that she appeared a bit perplexed. His steps slowed as he approached the counter and he looked at them, one after the other.

"What's the matter, May-May?" he finally asked.

She looked at her twin and smiled, her anger having been spent and her mood restored. "Nothing, why?" Squeezing out the dishcloth, she shut off the water and turned around to wipe down the counter on the opposite side of the kitchen.

Mike glanced at Scott, but the latter was still watching Mabel, holding back a joyous shout of laughter that wanted to bubble forth from his chest. Then Scott shook his head and looked at Mike, accepting the bills that were handed to him. Scott stuck the cash in his back pocket, drained his coffee mug, and then set the mug in the sink.

"Ready whenever you are, bro," he said casually.

"Great, I'll get my boots," Mike said, heading to the mudroom. "See you, May. Save some coffeecake for us!"

"Have fun," she called after them, turning back to the sink. Then she noticed that Scott had paused in the hallway and was looking back at her.

"One thing," he said, and she was forced to face his kind blue eyes again. "I agree with you. I prefer to just be friends and see what happens," he said steadily, smiling once more before leaving with Mike.

Mabel was inclined to feel extremely annoyed by his agreeable response and his pleasant attitude, but as the morning wore on, her irritation gradually dissipated. By the time the family got up and Mike and Scott returned, she was sufficiently subdued to be friendly to Scott and she even enjoyed getting to know him over lunch.

Later on that night, after the busy day had finally wound down, Mabel was contentedly dozing over her French handbook at her desk when Mike knocked on the bedroom door.

"Go away!" June yelled in a shrill tone, pulling her pajama shirt over her head. "It's bedtime!"

"I just wanna talk to May!" he yelled back through the door, imitating her tone.

Mabel laughed and got up, going out into the hallway with her finger still stuck in her book. "Yes?" she said suspiciously. "What do you want, brother dear?"

"What's your problem with Scott?" he said directly without introduction.

"I don't have a problem," she said, immediately blushing. "Who said I have a problem?"

"He said you yelled at him," Mike said, appearing perplexed. "He thought it was funny, but I don't. He's a good friend of mine, and he's a good guy, as decent as they come. So, what's your issue?"

"Nothing," she insisted, still blushing, "I was just overreacting." Realizing that was not enough of an explanation, Mabel added, "I didn't know why he showed up, so I thought he was another Richard P. Brighton."

"You're kidding me," Mike said, truly annoyed.

She blushed even redder. "Okay! I'm sorry! But I didn't know!"

"He's nothing of the sort. They're not even on the same level."

"Please, don't be mad," Mabel said, now truly apologetic. "I know I was wrong, so please don't yell at me. I figured out pretty fast he's a good guy, and it was dumb of me to yell at him." She looked up at her brother tentatively. "Are you still mad at me?"

"No, it's okay, as infuriating as you can be," Mike said, shaking his head and letting out a deep breath. "But really, how many times have I told you, you don't need to be so dramatic and uptight about life, about every guy you meet, or about anything!"

"I know, I know," his sister said dismissively, turning back to her room.

Letting out a grunt of frustration, he added, "If you didn't hate Scott that much, I would even think you two could be good friends and maybe even get married one day." He looked at her sharply and swiftly added before she could react, "Your personalities would go well together, and he said he liked you, but don't let that bother you. He said he wouldn't ask you out unless you were interested."

When Mabel turned back and stared at her brother, Mike looked puzzled. "Now what?"

"Do you really think that? Did Scott really say that?"

"Yes," he said dryly. "When do I ever say things I don't mean?"

"Rarely," Mabel admitted. "But—if Scott is *your* friend, I wouldn't want to take him away from you or anything."

"Good grief, it doesn't work like that!" Mike said explosively. "Where did you get that dumb idea?"

"I don't know," she said, appearing embarrassed again. "But—seriously, are you saying you wouldn't care if he asked me out or something?"

"Not at all," Mike said, a bit calmer this time. Seeing how her face began to look sad, he said, "Now what? You don't have to go out with him if you don't want to!"

"It's not that," May said, looking up at her brother. "But supposing that it did work out, I mean, if Scott did like me and we started dating, that's nice for me, but what about you, Mikey?"

"What about me?" he wondered.

"Well, I always had this idea that since we're so close that if one started getting in a relationship, then the other would, too. So, what about you? You might be sad and lonely!"

"Oh my goodness!" Mike burst out in exasperation, flailing his arms about as if he would punch her, though she knew that he would not and did not even flinch. "Seriously, May-May, what have you been reading and what have you been listening to? Give me that book!"

"It's just language study!" she said, holding up her French book to show him before he had a chance to wrest it away.

"That's your problem!" he said snidely. "French! You should have studied German instead!"

Shoving him aside and ignoring that slight, she peered up into her brother's face. "Do you really think I'm that ridiculous? Scott said that you said that I was feisty. What is that supposed to mean?"

"Feisty is the word," he said with a twinkle in his eye, and then he ran down the hall away from her before she had a chance to smack him with the book. Her only recourse was to stick her tongue out at her brother as he chuckled his way to his own room.

But May was content, Mike was satisfied, and the world was full of love.

CHAPTER FOURTEEN

The Coffeeshop

The bell on the door tinkled gently, and the coffee shop owner glanced up to greet the next customer. He smiled grimly as the woman brushed stray locks of dirty blonde hair from her forehead and approached the counter, lips pursed.

It was her again, and Sam already knew the order.

"Medium chai, please," she said in a peculiarly strong voice for such a small woman with such an uneasy appearance, as if she had a wary habit of looking out for danger. "For here."

"Three forty-five," he said automatically, nodding at the boy to his right to start up the machine. It always took a real man to make a good strong chai, Sam believed, but it didn't hurt for the tall, lanky kid to have some practice. He scooped out the change for her five-dollar bill and then eyed her skeptically as she retreated to the back table by the window, sat down, and opened a spiral-bound notebook.

The first time Sam saw her, he thought she was some snoop from the press. Yet, she had asked no questions, talked to no one on his staff, and simply sat wide-eyed by the big window the whole while. Occasionally, she stopped her staring to begin scribbling in that book of hers. When she had finally picked up her forgotten cup of chai, Sam labeled her a lost and searching soul and left it at that. She came back again and again, and he never changed his opinion of her.

She was, after all, just one of the many lost and searching souls in the little drifting village. They were all artsy folks and nomadic seekers, pushing out the steady farmers and determined craftsmen. What was the world coming to?

Sam turned away from the counter to see the awkward teen finishing up the chai. He squinted his eyes critically for a moment when the young man held it out in his direction.

"All right, fine," he said gruffly, finished with his visual inspection. He picked up his clipboard from the counter and turned toward the back to check the stock of coffee.

"Mr. Lambert?" the kid called him back, but Sam didn't flinch.

"It's for the crazy woman near the window."

The boy, Jeff, turned three shades of red but managed to stagger his way around the counter and across the room toward her table with the cup balanced on a saucer. He racked his brain for a polite greeting or a witty statement, but when she smiled at him gratefully, he lost his wits and remained tongue-tied.

On his way back to the register, Jeff inadvertently bumped into two chairs and one table, so he spent several minutes wiping down surfaces that had already been cleaned thirty minutes ago. Having successfully returned to the counter without further mishaps, the boy glanced around and slipped up on his barstool perch with relief.

It was a quiet Tuesday afternoon, and the only other people in the establishment were two chatty elderly women who came for tea once a week around two o'clock. Jeff sighed, glancing at the clock. Two-forty-two, and he was here until Sam closed at seven.

Jeff cast a timid look at the woman, but seeing that she paid him no mind, his stare gradually became bolder. She looked rather tired and lonely, and as far as he knew from her frequent visits to the coffee shop, she always was like that.

He felt the sudden urge to go give her a sweetmeat. Something to cheer her up, perhaps. An inner dialogue began under the raggedy mop of his dark brown hair.

A cookie? Too plain for someone as pretty as her. A sweet roll? It would not go with the chai. Cake? Pie? Sam would never approve of such an expensive donation. Perhaps biscotti? Yes, the old traditional sweet that went well with all hot drinks. Yes, that would have to do.

Glancing toward the back, Jeff hopped off the stool, knowing Sam was still busy prepping the back room while waiting for the weekly supply delivery to show up.

The awkward young man suddenly felt gallant and affable. Sweeping over to the biscotti jars, Jeff snatched up a crinkly tissue, popped off the lid from the nearest one, and plunged his hand inside. He felt triumphant and grinned to himself as the biscotti emerged, crumbs hopping off when he tapped the sweetmeat gently against the side of the jar.

A few seconds later, Jeff was walking back toward her table, his knees beginning to shake.

"Ex-excuse me."

She glanced up, pen poised above her notebook, a guarded look on her face.

"Would you like a-a-a biscotti? They go w-wonderful well wi-with chai."

She smiled, a sweet dimple appearing in one cheek, and the usual hardness in her eyes disappearing. "Oh, thank you, but I'm afraid I can't."

Jeff looked crestfallen, and he froze as he stood there, leaning over slightly for the dramatic moment when he would sweep out a fancy napkin and lay it down with a flourish, the prepared biscotti carefully clutched in his other hand. "Wh-why not?"

"I'm nut-free."

Immediately, he beamed. "Oh, bu-but you see, these *are* nut-free. They only have ch-chocolate chips."

"Oh." She smiled again, bemused. "Well, if you say so, then, sure. Thank you." She watched as his moment of truth arrived, the fancy napkin appeared with a flourish, and the biscotti gallantly descended to rest upon the table in front of her.

"There you are," he said, standing upright with an awkward grin.

"Thank you," she said again, the bemused expression still upon her face as she glanced out the window, willing him to leave.

"Anytime, miss—what is your name?"

Her eyebrows rose upon hearing the hint of desperation in his tone. "Ellen," she finally answered after a skeptical look back in his direction.

"Ellen." He beamed and then opened his mouth again to share his own name.

"Jeff!" Sam boomed in a faraway tone from the back.

"Yeah, I'm Jeff." The crestfallen look reappeared on his face. "I-I gotta go. N-nice to meet you, Ellen."

"Yes, nice to meet you, too, Jeff," she said simply, turning back to her book and rolling her eyes to herself. Before the young man had crossed the floor, she had already disappeared into her own little world and did not even notice that he had successfully returned to the counter, narrowly missing another couple of chairs and several tables.

The boy was gone, that was what mattered. Ellen sighed deeply with discomfort, almost with disgust. It was not that Jeff himself was repulsive. He was, after all, a human being and just a bumbling boy at that. Her weariness in regard to him had nothing to do with the fact that he was awkward or young. The problem was simply that she wanted to be left alone.

Ellen sighed again and stared out the window at the passing cars and sidewalk scattered with people.

It had not always been like this, of course. Two years ago, she had been at the height of a wild and busy career with the love life and social circles to match, and she had been very happy with that lifestyle. Yes, she had been exceedingly happy, even drunken with happiness. But now, she was tired, lonely, and burned out. Life had offered her grapes, and she had not the skill, courage, or fortitude to make wine. So, as the natural process would have it, her crushed grapes turned into sour vinegar.

Wearily, the woman picked up the biscotti and bit into it. She chewed slowly, deep in her own thoughts. How long had it been since she had longed to find her answer to life? It was now approaching three years since she freed herself from the corporate hustle, separated from her devoted Romeo, and disappeared from the social scene. Today, she was no more enlightened than the day she had deliberately put an end to it all.

Shifting in her seat with yet another sigh, Ellen turned to glance at the jangling door as a fashionable young couple walked in. She watched them saunter their way to the counter, appearing full of youthful vigor and the happiness of thoughtless passion.

Feeling bewildered, Ellen picked up her pen once more and scribbled down one last thought for the afternoon.

"The world is full of love—"

She paused to tap the word love with her pen-point, glancing up again at the couple in front of the counter. Shaking her head to see how they leaned against each other heavily with their arms locked together, she glanced instead at the biscotti. Was it merely a token or so much more?

Ellen looked out the window to see the clouds drifting by, revealing sunny skies beyond Main Street's tree line. Again, she bent over the notebook.

"—and all I have to do is embrace it."

Clicking the pen shut, she shoved it and the notebook into her purse. Rising, the woman glanced around the coffee shop once before straightening and turning her back on the finished chai, the half-eaten biscotti, and another five-dollar bill hidden beneath Jeff's fancy napkin.

Please Leave a Review

If you enjoyed reading *Faithless Friends and Replacement Lovers*, then please be kind and leave a review on the site from which you purchased the book. Book reviews greatly help both authors and readers, and I look forward to hearing what you thought about my collection!

Read More

Before you go, check out the following sample from my first book, ***Adventures Are Everywhere: Short Stories for the Explorer at Heart***, available on Amazon and other major online distributors.

ROBBERY AT DOONESVILLE

It was a dry and windy Sunday morning in the southern part of Doonesville. The whole town's population of forty-two people had turned out early, and forty-one of those souls were now sitting in the meetinghouse at the center of town, listening to the circuit rider Father Brown preach mightily in the pulpit. An occasional "Amen" came from the graybeards in the far right corner, but for the most part, the congregants were silent and still in their pews.

The only soul not in attendance for Sunday's meeting was an old reprobate sitting on the stoop in front of the general store. He shifted a bit in his baggy brown trousers and leaned his matted gray head against the porch railing as a dust cloud began to gather at the head of Main Street. Sighing with the wind, he tilted his grizzled chin back and began to let out the quavering beginnings of an old sailor's tune.

"Fifteen men on the dead man's—"

His voice trailed off as the cause of the dust cloud became apparent. Two riders were steadily making their way down the street past his stoop, headed directly toward the meetinghouse. Sitting up straight, the reprobate followed the strange men with his eyes, noting their old clothes, their ratty hats, and their tired horses. He craned his neck all the way around to watch them until they disappeared around the corner of the large white building.

"Trouble," muttered the old man, leaning back again and shaking his head. "No good." Sighing again, he folded his arms across his chest to ward off the brisk wind that swept along the road in front of him.

"Must be the whiskey." Eying the empty bottle that sat on the steps beside him, he shook his head again and resumed his toneless warbling, completely dismissing the sight of the two riders from his memory.

Around the corner of the meetinghouse, the two newcomers dismounted from their steeds and tied the reins to the hitching rail alongside several other horses and a couple of carriages. After a brief consultation, they nodded in agreement, removed their dusty hats, and began to rustle in their saddlebags for holier garb.

"Do you s'pose the old reverend is done yappin' by now?" Frederick asked, looking down his crooked nose at his companion before disappearing as he pulled a black robe over his head.

"'Spect so," Oscar replied. "Filcher tole me he'd be done promptly at 9:45, and here it's 'most 10."

The latter speaker pulled a beat-up timepiece from his front pocket and eyed it a moment before holding it up to his ear. Hearing nothing, he shook it a bit, took another listen, and then replaced it in his shirt with a careless shrug.

Glancing up at the sun and then down at his shadow, Oscar nodded to Frederick with confidence.

"Then let's go," Fred growled, straightening the ratty cloak around his shoulders and turning to see his friend doing likewise with his own robe.

The two travelers met Deacon Strong in the alcove, finding him neatly replacing a stick with a rabbit's foot in its special ledge by the bell pull trapdoor.

"Ahhh," the deacon breathed a wispy greeting, clasping his hands in front of him and bowing slightly. Whether he was nervous, uneasy, or simply startled, the men did not know, but they imitated his peculiar behavior by also clasping their hands in front of their own robes and bowing back.

In actuality, Deacon Strong was giddy with delight. It was collection day at the parish and the poor box was simply brimming over with generous gifts. His busy mind had been occupied all sermon with purchases for the needy and improvements to the building. Now, unclasping his hands, he motioned the men to follow him as he opened the sanctuary doors before them.

As the three crossed the threshold, the parish man swiftly surveyed the congregation, wondering how to seat the two men in such a way that it would add to the harmony of the church and not cause the least bit of division. At the same time, Deacon Strong noticed that Father Brown was just returning the cup to its place on the communion table and dearly hoped that the newcomers would not disrupt the meditative mood of the service.

Before the deacon had a chance for his worry to set in, Father Brown turned to face the congregation, lifting his hands to pray a simple two-line blessing.

"Amen," all the people responded, and Frederick and Oscar eagerly echoed the word, causing Deacon Strong's heart to swell with happiness that the travelers were doing their part to fit in with the assembly. Clasping his hands together once more, he bowed his head in solemn and reverent prayer.

As if on cue, the old pump organ began to wheeze out an eerie tune and all the people stood in unison to sing. Presently, the instrument came to life with a rush and hastened to catch up with the voices, the blended sounds creating a glorious symphony that reached into the rafters before filling the entire building.

Slowly, the voices began to fade one by one as astonished eyes met the sight of a black-robed figure solemnly parading up the aisle toward Father Brown. By the time a second figure appeared in a dingy blue robe, all the congregants were simply standing there with their mouths agape. The only remaining sounds came from the pump organ and Father Brown, who shared a holy "Amen" before also coming to a rest.

Father Brown raised his bespectacled face from the Psalm book and lowered his conducting arm to find himself flanked by two strange men. He blinked in surprise as the taller man in the black robe stepped forward to shake his hand vigorously. Then the stranger turned toward the pulpit, lifted down the poor box, tucked it under his arm, and spun about on his heel to march down the aisle.

Before anyone could raise a note of protest, the shorter man in the blue robe also stepped forward and took Father Brown's hand in both of his in an apparent move of joy and thanksgiving. Turning toward the congregation and lifting Father Brown's arm in a movement of celebration and praise, he began the following prayer:

"We praise Thee, O Lor' our Father, for Thy generosity an' goodness that these gifts shalt verily bless Thy poor people of Shaftesbury who suffereth from a ragin' fire."

A great gasp was heard through the room at this juncture and many a compassionate head was shaken in pity as the speaker continued unabated.

"An' we thank Thee, O God our Lor', for these good folks who giveth abundantly at all times. So let all people that on earth do dwell sing praise to Thee, a hundred times o'er."

With a hearty "Amen and amen," the organist and Father Brown immediately took the cue and began to lead the singing of the Old Hundredth.

The building shook with fervor as the blue-robed man walked back down the aisle in a great meditative state to meet his companion who was busily bowing to and wringing the hand of Deacon Strong. By the time the song ended, the men were on their way. The wind blew the door shut, leaving the deacon all alone in the alcove to adjust the tuft of hair on his head.

Father Brown set down his Psalm book and lifted his hands to pray over the people one last time before delivering the benediction. All heads dutifully bowed in response, except for one that belonged to a certain man by the name of Albert Jenkins.

This fellow carefully scanned the small crowd suspiciously until the last "Amen" was pronounced. Then he skirted the little groups of congregants as they busily gathered around the Father. He plucked the sleeve of another young man who stood near a group seeking to console Deacon Strong in his grief over the plight of Shaftesbury. The furrow in Albert's brow smoothed when he saw the thoughtful look on the face of his friend.

"You thinkin' what I be thinkin'?" Albert wondered as the two of them escaped the hot confines of the meetinghouse and headed for their horses.

Read ***Adventures Are Everywhere: Short Stories for the Explorer at Heart*** to learn what happens next!

About the Author

The author manages Elizabeth's Writing Corner, where she coaches aspiring authors and helps them publish their own books. Her favorite pastime is spending time with her boys and telling them stories about the world. Elizabeth enjoys meeting people from all around the world and would gladly connect with you on social media or through her website at https://www.elizabeths writingcorner.com.